SHADOW ROCK

**A REN COPELAND
INVESTIGATION**

Alex Nichols

ZOOEYCOPE BOOKS

SHADOW ROCK

zooeycope books

ISBN 978-1735703527

Cover Art and Design by Danitsa Janssen

ACKNOWLEDGEMENTS

Special thanks to Detective Floyd Mohr (retired, Glencoe, IL Police Department) for vetting the manuscript. Additional thanks to Caren Estesen, Elizabeth Pomada, and Dee Mura for offering useful feedback along the way.

for kellee

CHAPTER ONE

Lydia Merton was thirty-three years old before she saw a corpse for the first time. Unlike professionals in forensics or grieving relatives at morgues, she was wholly unprepared for the shock of seeing a dead girl. It was not that death and loss had eluded Lydia up until that point; most of her family by then was scattered ashes. What had surprised her was that the corpse was in her house.

It all began on a chilly day in October. Lydia sat, legs crossed, listening to the whir of the jet engine as it began its descent. A Xanax stained her tongue, settling her nerves as the plane passed through cloud cover. Her arms were long and thin, branch-like, reaching out from her slender body.

A flight attendant darted through the cabin, collecting litter and distributing landing cards. She advised a harried mother to put her hopping son into a seat belt. A distinguished looking man turned pages on a broadsheet. A boy with shaggy curls and a beard of acne pulled at his earphones. Thirty thousand feet and a blanket of autumn clouds above Sea-Tac Airport, this could have been a group of travelers arriving anywhere.

Lydia closed her eyes and imagined the week that lay ahead of her. Next Monday it was back to work, a return crop of bored and angsty students daydreaming away her lectures. She pictured the long, nondescript corridors that lead to her classroom and to her boxy, stale office. She visualized a stack of papers, indistinguishable year after year. She saw herself, bone tired, getting on the bus at the end of her week. The bus driver's sad, weary smile as he greeted her: "Miss Merton, you're like clockwork."

To cheer herself up, Lydia thought about the previous days. Deer Lodge had a Narnia-like splendor, built as it was amidst jagged snowy peaks and turquoise waters. The inky night skies held a patchwork of stars: points of light spelling out the future. The awe was with her still. Her thin lips crinkled into a smile. She could live for a while off the memories.

The plane skidded slightly as it hit the tarmac, landing with a reassuring thud. No matter the pleasures of the previous days, Lydia was glad that she wouldn't be flying again any time soon. She didn't like being airborne: the feeling of utter defenselessness when up against the cruelty of fate. Only fools believed they would be spared bad luck.

Lydia collected her things and exited the plane. Now that she was home, she could fall back into her routine: a leisurely morning, class in the afternoon and some evenings, dinner and TiVo at night; chores and paper grading on Saturdays; a luxurious Sunday with buttermilk waffles and the *New York Times*. She had a nice life, Lydia told herself. Many would kill for it.

She moved through the passport check with a quick grace and was among the first from her flight at the baggage claim. A crowd gathered around the carousel, chatting animatedly as the conveyer belt began to churn. There were families and business travelers and a small group of Buddhist monks, fat and happy in their saffron robes.

As she watched luggage drop from the chute, Lydia was aware of a man standing behind her. He was tall, almost casting a shadow over her. He had been on her flight, sitting a few rows behind her. He had a shaved head with visible gray stubble at his temples and large, dark eyes. Lydia turned her head to the side, catching him briefly in her vision. After a moment, she moved away to the other side of the carousel. The man was still there, looking at her.

Lydia continued her solitary wait. Why was it that her bag

never failed to be among the last removed from the plane? She fished into her sweater for a phone. She turned it on, typed something, and slipped it back into her pocket.

At last, her black Eddie Bauer suitcase came into view. She moved over to meet it, pulled the handle up, and exited past the customs agent, handing him her landing card as she went. She had nothing to declare. She walked with purpose back into the main lobby and left the airport, bracing herself against a cold north wind.

Inside the terminal, the man from Lydia's flight was still at baggage claim. His phone was in his hand, a text message still in view:

> *don't stare at me. people will notice.*

It was from Lydia.

CHAPTER TWO

Lydia exited the bus at Aloha. This was her usual stop: her house was across 23rd Avenue and up a small hill. Holy Names Academy was ahead, its dome and cross visible for blocks. Behind her as she climbed, the Cascades faded from view as dusk settled over Capitol Hill. The weather had cleared since landing, and there was a brisk, fresh quality to the air. It was kelp and sea salt and the promise of winter.

Lydia moved slowly, the wheels on her bag dragging against the pavement. Soon it would be dark. She tried to remember what food she had in the house and what she would need to buy. Milk and cream certainly, and possibly coffee beans. She would make a run to QFC on 15th after she dropped off her stuff. It was Thursday, and she had the long weekend to get caught up on the things she had neglected to do while in Alberta.

Lydia fished her phone out of her sweater pocket and glanced at it. No word back yet from David. This wasn't surprising. In the years they had been together, Lydia had yet to fully understand David's temperament or even his schedule. There were no set times that she could expect a phone call, no offhand comments she could make knowing what his reaction would be. He was, if nothing else, a bit of a puzzle. Perhaps this was one reason their relationship had lasted so long. Lydia didn't like to be bored. With David, she never was.

Lydia stopped for a moment outside her house. Wind rustled through the trees that towered over her. She shivered a bit as a few stray drops of water fell from the branches above.

She typed a message to David and sent it:

hope I wasn't too harsh. you know the rules.

She moved onto her porch. A small stack of mail was wedged into her box, so far down she had to swipe her hand low to pull it out. It was the usual: catalogs and bills, a notice from her dentist that it was time to get her teeth cleaned.

Lydia turned the key in the lock. She was exhausted, sleep-walking. She felt lightheaded and forgetful. All she wanted was to go to bed. She flipped the living room lights on.

Things always seemed a bit disorienting to her when she got back from a trip. The ceilings seemed higher, the walls brighter. Lydia couldn't remember having left out the quilt that was on her couch. The bookshelf doors were ajar…had she grabbed a book on her way out? When she moved to the dining room it was more familiar. She had left out some linen that needed to be ironed, along with some candlesticks that needed polishing.

It was in the kitchen that Lydia began to feel odd. It occurred to her how cold it was in her house; it felt like a meat locker. There was a metallic smell that she noticed but couldn't immediately isolate.

A door separated the kitchen from the basement stairs, and she saw now that it was unlatched. Normally it locked automatically, keeping the basement separate from the rest of the house. She must have forgotten to shut it properly on her way out the previous Saturday. That made sense to her. She had left in haste and had even forgotten the printout for her boarding pass and a receipt she had needed for her rental car. She had left without her winter coat as well, rushing off in a sweater that had seemed threadbare once she reached the mountain air. Lydia remembered all that now.

A comforting thought hit her: *maybe it was just Hector.* Hector came by every few weeks to tend to the lawn and garden and assisted with general upkeep of the property. She had mentioned to him the last time they spoke that the gutters needed to be cleared and that she would be gone for a few days. He had a key to the basement door, so he could get to supplies in the workroom. It was possible he had come upstairs for a bit.

It's OK, Lydia thought. Hector is a family man, a grandfather. Who would begrudge him a look around? Maybe he took a break on the clock. She would talk to him about it, or maybe she would just let it slide. Everybody needed a day off occasionally.

Lydia took a bottle of water from the fridge and drank from it. She was always thirsty after a flight. She looked at herself in the reflection of the window over the sink. She felt a chill again, a fear she sometimes felt alone in the house after dark. She set the bottle down on the counter, and moved into the TV room.

It was then that Lydia saw the body.

CHAPTER THREE

Detective Ren Copeland had been fat as a kid, and she still walked with a loping gait. Or at least it felt that way to her as she moved across the padded floors at the Lone Wolf Self Defense Center in Skyway. She was learning Kajukenbo, a martial art that was supposed to help with balance and fluidity. Thus far in her training, she had never felt more clumsy. Her sifu was a lithe hapa woman, and Ren flushed every time the instructor focused attention on her. She felt awkward and gawky around her. What she wouldn't give to command her body the way Sifu Pearl did.

Ren couldn't quite shake the feeling of inadequacy as she headed home. Ahead of her as she drove, Seattle glittered in the night air. The Space Needle was lit up, a soldier guarding Elliott Bay. On the radio, some sixteen-year-old with fake tits and sharp nails was singing that the only person you need to love is yourself.

Ren's car was a vintage turquoise Camaro, more sport than muscle. It was a gift from one of her mother's boyfriends. In the mid '90s he had been angling to be Ren's stepfather and had surprised her with the gift when she turned seventeen. The car was all that remained of him.

Ren had promised her brother that she would stop by Sanctuary, his bar in Pioneer Square. Ramon was just back from a cooking seminar in Provence and was excited about introducing some food items to the menu. Ren was looking forward to her favorite cocktail, a mix of lime sorbet and liquor. She could almost taste the icy citrus slush as she drove. When her phone rang, she knew she was running late. When it wasn't the ring tone she was expecting, she knew something was up.

"You're not going to believe this, Ren; some woman is in hot water. Claims she found a dead body in her house. They just assigned us."

Sean Lukela, Ren's partner, was calling from a crime scene on Capitol Hill, not far from the Seattle East precinct. This was a neighborhood known for day spas and boulangeries. Ren and Sean had been paired for seven years, and no case they'd been assigned would ever be as easy a commute from the office. Ordinarily they worked missing persons cases. Homicide was rare.

Ren took the Olive Street exit and made her way to the scene. A fire truck and ambulance blocked the turn off Aloha, and squad cars crowded the area near the front lawn. Neighbors stood on porches under yellow light. As Ren approached the house, she saw the Crime Scene Unit signing in at the door with their tackle boxes. Ren waited for them to gain clearance before she ducked under the yellow tape. She found Sean standing in the kitchen talking into his cell phone. Ren gave her partner the once-over. He was wearing button flies and a hoodie.

"Lieutenant Roemer said she's coming back from maternity leave tomorrow," Sean said when he rang off. "She's not going to be able to make it to the scene tonight."

Poor Lieutenant Roemer. She had a five-week-old baby boy and an unexpected crime on her hands. Ren could only imagine what a mad scramble she was going through right now. It had raised a few eyebrows when the head of the Seattle East precinct had made the decision to become a single mother. It merely confirmed to some that women were not capable of being in charge. There was gossip that the head of CSU, Joshua Conlin, was angling for her job.

"You couldn't have dressed for the occasion?" Ren asked Sean as they moved through the kitchen to the back room.

"Look who's talking," Sean said, surveying her yoga pants and puffy jacket. "Besides I beat you by ten minutes. Where the hell were you?"

It was a reasonable question, as Ren lived not far from here. Like any good detective, she knew not to answer questions that might lead to more questions.

The walls of the back room were painted tortoise shell green. There was a Navajo tapestry hanging on one. This made the sight of a corpse on the floor all the more jarring. It was a young woman, lying on her back. Her eyes were open, staring at the ceiling. A large puddle of blood had pooled around her head. She was dressed in jeans and a Grateful Dead tee, and had fringe moccasin boots on her feet. When Ren looked closely at her, she saw a gold hoop earring in her left nostril and a sprinkling of freckles across her nose.

There was a sharp metallic smell, as well as a pungent smell of stale garlic. It had been a long time since Ren had been this close to death.

"The owner of the house claims to have found the body when she returned from a trip tonight. There are signs of a break-in downstairs. The social worker is talking to her right now."

Ren nodded. She had seen them when she arrived.

The CSU team had begun to take over, led by Joshua Conlin. He was a slight man with John Lennon–style spectacles and a thin ponytail that snaked down his back like a tributary. He barked orders and micromanaged in a way that bordered on petty. He had been the acting head of Seattle East for the six weeks that Lieutenant Roemer was on leave. Ren had been counting the minutes until he went back where he belonged.

"I need to secure this scene. Get back," he yapped at them, and Ren and Sean stepped back into the kitchen.

"I see that Big Swinging Dick is in da house," a woman said, just loud enough to risk being heard by the wrong person. Stella Hadley stepped into the kitchen and joined the detectives. She had been their classmate at the Academy years ago, before she switched to social work. Her personality was a bit too large for enclosed spaces, like a Macy's Parade balloon trapped indoors. That hadn't changed.

"I've spent the last fifteen minutes talking to Lydia," Stella told them. They could hear the Camel unfiltered in her voice. "She seems quite shaken up, but I think she's competent to endure an interview. I told her that she will likely be displaced for some time. She seems to understand that her house is now a crime scene."

The CSU team was working both in the back room where the body was found and in an area in the basement, where there was evidence of a break-in. The house was their domain as they dusted for fingerprints, arranged to remove the body, and looked for blood spatter and other DNA. A photographer's flash went off every few minutes as he documented the scene.

Ren made her way down a set of wooden steps to the basement. There was a washer and dryer in one corner, and a crowded workbench in another, as well as an old chrome bar set covered with empty boxes and packing peanuts. A CSU technician was focused on the area around the door, where a window had been broken. There were shards of glass on the floor, including one that seemed to have blood spatter on it.

"Any sign this was staged?" Ren asked him.

Henry Wu looked up from his work. "My initial impression is no. The window appears to have been broken from the outside, and the trajectory does not arouse suspicion."

All of this really meant nothing. Lydia Merton would be considered a suspect until they were able to clear her.

Joshua Conlin barreled down the stairs, emitting a blustery sound that was his idea of a greeting. "Detective, your suspect is standing alone on the front lawn. Is that wise?"

Ren bristled but resisted the urge to snap back at him. "We're about to head over to the precinct, sir. I anxiously await your report."

Henry Wu shot Ren a sympathetic look. They all labored under the burden of Joshua Conlin. This had been the hot topic the last time Ren met the CSU crew for margaritas at Bimbo's.

Ren did another sweep of the house, viewing the body one more time. She then joined Stella and Sean on the front lawn. They were standing with the owner of the house.

Ren gave Lydia a once over as she introduced herself. She had a stern brow and sharp nose, a look reminiscent of a Picasso painting Ren had once seen. She was rail thin and had a few strands of gray hair at her temples. Ren would be surprised later to learn that they were the same age. Lydia Merton gave off the aura of someone from a different era.

"My coat," Lydia said. These were her first words to Ren. "I keep asking people to get my winter coat from the closet inside. No one has done it."

Ren signaled to a patrol officer and took his bulky parka. She wrapped it around Lydia's shoulders. "My partner and I are going to want to talk to you tonight. I think we'll all be more comfortable at the precinct."

Lydia nodded. Ren hoped her taciturnity would disappear by the time they were in the interview room.

"I assume the social worker told you that you aren't going to have access to your house for the immediate future. You have somewhere you can stay, with a boyfriend or something?"

Lydia shook her head.

"We can put you up for the night. After that you're on your own."

Ren arranged to have a squad car transport Lydia to the precinct. She helped her into the backseat of the car. She didn't have to the heart to tell her that this was the best she was going to get for some time. Her house and its contents were now the sealed jurisdiction of King County Police.

It would be eight weeks before Lydia Merton would step foot in her house again.

CHAPTER FOUR

The quickest way to tick Detective Sean Lukela off was to remind him of his Academy nickname, Officer Hunk. He didn't like it, and he didn't get it: he considered himself average looking. When suspects opened their hearts to him, revealing information that others could never glean, he assumed it was because he was good at his job.

His partner, Ren Copeland, had had an Academy nickname too: Officer Fen Phen. She wasn't crazy about it herself. It didn't matter to some people how hard she'd worked to pass the physical. She would always be the woman who lost eighty pounds to cross the thin blue line. She had kept the weight off for fourteen years, but it didn't matter. There are things people don't want to forget.

They sat in Interview Room A at the Seattle East precinct. Across the table from them, Lydia Merton had produced a small heap of receipts from her recent trip: Hertz Rental Car at the Calgary Airport, the Deer Lodge at Lake Louise, stubs from an Air Canada flight arriving earlier that afternoon. Some junior detectives were currently confirming her alibi, and a document examiner was comparing the signatures on the customs forms she had signed at Sea Tac with the signature she had given them.

"You're sure you've never seen this girl before?" Ren asked, taking a moment to jot down a comment in her notepad. "You don't think it might be one of your students?"

Lydia shook her head and took a sip of cool water from a glass. She had told them about her job teaching comparative religion in the humanities department at Pacific Community College.

"Maybe she was connected to Holy Names," Lydia said. She was talking about an all-girls high school that was across from her house. "There are always students loitering around my street. Maybe she was watching the house and knew I was gone."

"I used to date a lady who taught at Holy Names," Sean said. "They had a nickname for it back then."

Horny Dames, Ren thought. She had seen Sean do this routine before. Build a rapport with an interview. Some ate straight from his hand.

"And my partner went to St. Veronica Preparatory, didn't you, Ren? Veronica Prep. A Jesuit education wasted in a life of police work."

Lydia wasn't engaging in this small talk. She looked strained as she took another sip of water.

"You didn't notice anything missing from your house?" Ren said. "Jewelry or cash stolen?"

"Honestly, I don't have much," Lydia replied. "I had my passport and my cards with me. I don't keep much cash at home."

They would have her do another sweep of the house in the morning: looking for stolen items and anything out of place. It was quite normal for people in shock to not notice things.

Above them, the overhead lights flashed once. Ren and Sean exchanged a glance. This was a private signal that someone was at the door with information. Ren politely excused herself. When she stepped outside the interview room, she found Detective Jason Twick waiting for her. He was five feet tall with two deformed ears that sprouted like mushrooms from the sides of his head. His chest looked like a suit of armor. Whenever Ren saw him, she thought of the Lollipop Kids from *The Wizard of Oz.*

"We've confirmed with Air Canada, Deer Lodge, and the document examiner. She was in Canada until a few hours ago."

Ren nodded her head, feeling somewhat relieved. Conlin had called earlier with his estimate on the girl's time of death, and it was probable that she had been dead at least twelve hours.

"My team is going to canvass Holy Names and the neighborhood starting in a few hours," Jason told her. "We'll check with UPS and the mail carrier. I'll have my first report for you by noon."

Ren opened her mouth to thank him but was interrupted by the vibration of her phone. She glanced at it. It was a text from Conlin. She stepped back into the interview room. Sean was reading his phone as she took a seat next to him.

"Lydia, we've just received word that a fingerprint has been isolated on your basement door. It doesn't match your print or the print of the girl. We're going to need a list of anyone who has access to your house via that entrance." Ren looked at her notepad. "You mentioned this man who does garden work for you, Hector Daniels. Is there anyone else you can think of that might have entered via the basement recently?"

Lydia thought of all the times David had used his key to enter via the basement door. She would come home from class to find him napping in the downstairs bedroom, or cooking a pot roast in the kitchen. She knew he was there when she stepped through the front door and heard *Abbey Road* on the stereo.

"No," Lydia told the detectives. "I can't think of anyone."

• • •

By the time the interview wrapped up, it was after midnight. The full weight of the evening started to hit Lydia as she arrived at her hotel. She snapped at the front desk clerk, her mind overwhelmed with what lay ahead. She had class on Monday. The detectives had told her that they would bring over her suitcase once the forensics unit had finished photographing the scene; most likely she would have it by the time she woke up. Still, Lydia's life had been irretrievably misplaced. She needed her clothes, her laptop. She felt suspended in time, the way she did on a long layover at an airport.

Once in her hotel room, she fell onto the bed, sobbing. It was a childlike cry that she hadn't let out since her mother's death, the feeling of being inconsolable and seeing no light at the end of the tunnel. She buried her head into the pillow, feeling repelled by its institutional blandness.

After she lay there a while, Lydia fished into her purse. The detectives had left their contact information with her. She fingered the cards, wondering if she should call one of them. She imagined Detective Copeland driving home, bleary eyed but hopping with information about the case. She wondered if Ren lived alone. She probably had some cute husband who took care of their baby.

Lydia felt a lump in her throat. It was two in the morning, and she was all alone in a hotel room. She dumped the contents of her purse on the bed: her cell phone, her keys, a book, her wallet, and a small coin purse where she stashed her Xanax.

She picked up the book and thumbed through it. It was the story of Siamese twins who grow up on a farm. She remembered reading the first few chapters in the airport, her nerves buzzing from excitement and fear of flying. Midway through a page was torn, from when Lydia jumped at turbulence. Toward the end, the pages were crisped from bathwater. Lydia had finished the novel in the luxury of the tub at Deer

Lodge at Lake Louise. She held the book close to her nose. She could almost smell the wood smoke and fresh mountain air.

Lydia reached for her phone and pressed speed dial. She didn't care how late it was. David was used to this. The phone rang a few times. That should have tipped Lydia off, but she wasn't thinking clearly. Eventually, a woman answered, sleepy. "Westside Home for Girls," she said.

Lydia blanched a bit. It was the hotline, which David's phone was forwarded to when he was asleep.

"I need to talk to David Skarda," Lydia said.

"It's an emergency?"

"Yes."

There was a long pause as Lydia waited on hold. The center didn't leave Muzak on the line. After a few minutes in a soundless tunnel, he answered. She felt like crying from relief, from the comfort of his familiar voice.

"This is Father David Skarda," he said.

CHAPTER FIVE

Lieutenant Camille Roemer examined Sophie the Giraffe and scowled. She already had two at home, and the sight of another on her oak desk at the Seattle East precinct made her testy. It was the note attached to the box that set her off: *A whole new life for you. J R Conlin.*

Goddamn Conlin, she thought. Camille was no fool. Joshua Conlin wanted her job. She shoved the box into her bottom desk drawer and composed herself. She had only been back at work a few days, but she was struggling to keep her head in the game.

Six weeks ago, Camille had given birth. Her son was bald like Picasso, so she named him Pablo. Her feet were still swollen to the size of hams. She hadn't slept more than two hours at a stretch in over a month. She had to suppress all that for now. While her new son slept at their home in Laurelhurst in the care of his Nepalese nanny, his mother had a murder to solve.

On her desk she had two reports from the Capitol Hill case. The preliminary medical examiner's report listed the cause of death as blunt trauma to the head, most likely from a fall. The girl had also been stabbed several times in the lower abdomen. There was no sign of sexual assault. Her last meal, spinach and pasta and cheese and bread, was found both in the contents of her stomach and on the floor of the crime scene. It appeared that she had been interrupted while eating takeout from Pagliacci Pizza on upper Broadway.

The other report was a summary of the case so far, submitted by Detective Ren Copeland. It started with a transcript of the interview she and Detective Sean Lukela had conducted with Lydia Merton the night the body was discovered, and it continued into all the information they had learned in the four days since the case had opened. Neighbors and staff at Holy Names Academy had been interviewed, and the area around the house had been canvassed for leads all the way down to the commercial district on upper Broadway. Detective Copeland had finished the report with her opinion that evidence thus far suggested that the girl had broken into Lydia Merton's house while she was away. Most likely the girl's assailant was someone she knew, possibly someone who was staying at the house with her. The detectives were now operating on the theory that the girl in Lydia Merton's house was homeless.

$$\bullet \quad \bullet \quad \bullet$$

Camille closed the report and reflected on it. As usual, Ren's report was clear as a bell. She appreciated the ease of the writing. It was a holdover from their days as students at St. Veronica Preparatory, an elite girls' school on Queen Anne, where the elements of composition had been drilled into them. They had been a few classes apart, but their alumnae connection bonded them. They were also the only two women of rank at Seattle East.

Camille was interrupted from her thoughts by the bleating of the intercom. She picked up her desk phone, a relic from the '80s. The receiver felt like a small barbell in her hand. "Nola, I told you this morning, why not just come into my office? I don't like talking on this thing."

Without a word, the line went dead. A moment later a small woman appeared at the door. She had the curvy physique of a '50s pinup and a mess of tangled blonde hair. She was wearing a pink vinyl tank top, a black plumed skirt, and motorcycle boots. When she moved, a bell rang in time to her steps. It was attached to a streak of pink that ran through her curls.

"Fiona Swift just called again," Nola told her boss. "Am I just supposed to keep making excuses until she stops?"

Fiona Swift was a local crime reporter who sometimes sold televised pieces to national news programs. Despite the generally low crime rate in King County, she managed to make a living as a freelance journalist, operating a small office near Pike Place Market.

"Did she mention why she was calling?"

"Something about the Antony Marlin verdict. But she also wanted to know about the Capitol Hill case."

Camille looked out her window at the street below. There was an old bank building that had been turned into a Tully's Coffee. Its ornate façade looked like a gilded birdcage. It would be so nice to be sitting there now, with Pablo asleep in his sling. "I'll handle her, Nola. Can you do me a favor and get me a vanilla latte from across the street? Also one of those pink frosted cookies if they have them."

Nola nodded and disappeared. Camille reached for her Rolodex and looked up a number.

Camille had mixed feelings about talking to the press, but Fiona had proven her integrity over their years together. She fashioned herself after an era when one's word meant something.

Fiona answered on the first ring. "Lieutenant, I am so happy to be hearing from you. How is Pablo?"

"He's fine, Fiona. Thank you for the spoon you sent."

Fiona had sent Camille a monogrammed piece of silver, along with a handwritten note on embossed paper when the baby was born.

"Did I tell you how much I admire the name? None of this Max and Romy business."

Camille laughed. "The first time he picks up a paintbrush,

I'll be convinced of the power of suggestion. Now, what may I help you with today?"

"I'm working on two projects. One is a narrative piece about the Antony Marlin trial. I'm pitching it, and I'd like to get a few quotes from you."

Antony Marlin was a First Hill resident who went ape shit after his girlfriend, wielding a gun in public and missing her by about seven feet. Unfortunately, the stray bullet hit a patron at a gay bar. The jury was currently in its sixth day of deliberations.

"Then there is this curious case on Capitol Hill," Fiona said. "I've hired a crew to shoot some footage. I think this might have legs." Camille could hear Fiona lighting a cigarette with her Zippo lighter. She took a drag and exhaled. "It's funny. I walk by these kids every day, with their body piercings and their junkyard dogs. Many reek of alcohol. I've never heard of one breaking into someone's house. Might be a tidbit for the Swifters." Fiona had a group of acolytes who followed her every byline and even congregated online. Camille lurked on the website occasionally.

"Obviously it's an open case, so I can't comment on it. I'd be happy to give you some stock answers for the Marlin verdict if you're on deadline."

"Great. Let's do that," Fiona said. "But first this other case. Lydia Merton seems to be an interesting subject. I might be able to pitch this to homeowner's fears. I was thinking about it, alone at home last night. Is there any greater fear inducer to a woman than your space being invaded like that?"

Camille stayed silent.

"Do you think maybe she was caught unawares and killed an intruder? Some kind of primal killing that she is now covering up?"

"We will go where the evidence leads us."

"And then there is the fact that the house is opposite Holy Names Academy. Strictly between you and me, I've heard things about a few of the faculty there. I've got some inside information."

"Well, I certainly hope you will report anything to us that you uncover."

Nola appeared at the door with a cup of coffee and small paper bag. She deposited them in front of Camille. Camille took a sip of warm, frothy milk mixed with vanilla syrup and espresso. She reached into the bag and took a bite: a sugar cookie with sweet pink frosting. She felt transported.

"It is strange, though," Fiona was saying. "What are the odds that you would find a dead body in your house and not have any connection to it?"

Camille swallowed. Fiona's workday must involve many such one-sided conversations. She was probably used to the static silence following her leading questions.

"It's certainly got me thinking. But while I have you, let me get those Antony Marlin quotes. My pieces are always helped along by your thumbprint."

Camille could swear at times Fiona Swift was coming on to her. She had an obsequiousness that bordered on sapphic. Camille complied with her request, giving two opposing statements that Fiona could print, depending on the outcome of the verdict. She then offered a third, in case there was a mistrial.

"That's great, lieutenant. I really appreciate it. Also, strictly between you and me, I wanted to tell you something."

She paused dramatically, the same way she did in her televised pieces. "I play mah-jongg with a group of women. They're all gossips and gadabouts. I don't like any of them. But one of the ladies is friends with Joshua Conlin's mother."

Camille felt a chill dread, the kind that preceded a revelation she knew to be true but didn't want to acknowledge. She listened to what Fiona had to say. When Camille spoke again, it was with a sharp resolve. "That is absolutely not true, Fiona. I would laugh if it weren't such an undignified accusation. Now if you'll excuse me, I have work to do."

Camille rang off and sat in silence for a few moments. Outside her window a steady stream of traffic moved in time with the stoplights. A jackhammer riveted through concrete.

When Camille stood up, she grabbed her coffee and her half-eaten cookie. She stepped away from her desk, and then reconsidered and moved back. She opened the bottom drawer and pulled out Sophie the Giraffe, still in its packaging. The gift card was still attached. Walking to the exit, she threw the toy in the trash.

CHAPTER SIX

Detective Sean Lukela sat opposite the statue of the Virgin, feeling queasy. Religious iconography did that to him at times. The Blessed Mother was on a pedestal, draped in a periwinkle cloak covered in stars. Images of his boyhood visits to Moloka'i and the abandoned leper colonies lurked like ghosts in Sean's mind. They had been lurking all morning.

He shook the feeling away. The Westside Home for Girls was his fifth stop of the day, and he was looking forward to being done with it. It was run by the Roman Catholic Church, and in the past would have been known as a home for unwed mothers, focusing as it did on young women in crisis. Sean had lost count of the number of programs like this he had visited in the last two days. Seattle had a considerable homeless population. Children from intolerable living conditions left the hinterlands of eastern Washington to take their chances on the streets. The city had nearly a dozen programs to aid these kids.

The medical examiner had released a preliminary report, determining that the girl in Lydia Merton's house had died from blunt trauma to the head. A full autopsy, with toxicology results, would take a few weeks. Forensic analysis from the house showed little evidence left behind by the girl's attacker, and a canvass of the neighborhood down to Broadway yielded few results. Hector Daniels, a yardman for Lydia Merton, was fully vetted and cleared. He had not been by the house while Lydia was away. Examination of the DVR showed that several episodes of *True Blood* had been viewed while Lydia was in Alberta. Her alibi was rock solid. The police were operating on the theory that the girl in Lydia's house was homeless and had broken into the vacant house for a respite. This meant the odds were good she had looked to social services at some point.

Sean shifted his weight in the cracked vinyl sofa. He cast a baleful glance toward the woman sitting behind a desk a few feet away from him. Her nameplate read *Daphne Downey*. When he had arrived ten minutes before, she had disappeared behind a frosted amber glass door behind her desk. He could see her figure through the door, her hands gesticulating as she talked to someone.

"Do you mind taking a seat?" she asked him when she emerged again. "Sister Betty is on the phone with a client right now and will be out to meet you as soon as she can."

• • •

That was too long ago now. Sean had things to do. He cleared his throat and checked his watch, hoping to convey his impatience. Across the way was a dining hall. Sean could hear sounds of the kitchen staff: spraying water and industrial-sized pans being moved about. To the left of the dining room was a large, open room that looked like it had once been a gym. Down the hall there was a wide-set staircase leading to a second floor. The hallway was drab, a faded mustard color. Sean could smell baked beans.

At last, a slender woman appeared from behind the frosted amber office door. She was dressed in a gray skirt, a white shirt, and a blue headscarf. She was wearing white nurse's shoes that barely made a sound as she moved down the corridor to greet her guest. She introduced herself and ushered Sean back to her office. He took a seat on a vinyl chair that matched the sofa in the hallway.

"I assume you're familiar with the Capitol Hill case," he began. "I am investigating a death."

"I've heard of it, yes," Sister Betty said. "Young woman

stabbed to death. They think she was homeless and had broken into the property."

"That's right," Sean replied. Clearly she had been watching the news. "We are talking to all the social services that deal with runaways. We're trying to see if maybe she had come to you first, perhaps even stayed with you for a time."

Sister Betty explained the way Westside worked: It was both a residence for at risk youth and a temporary shelter for those needing a bed and two meals. There were fifteen beds available for long-term stay, and the overnight program ran about fifty a night. The overnight program alternated with four other churches and one synagogue, so the Westside Home only hosted the short-term crowd twice a year. This year April and December were their months to host. Sister Betty was familiar with the long-term residents but said it would be harder to speculate about short-term guests; it had been over six months since they'd hosted any.

Sean could see signs of strain in Sister Betty's face. This was tough work, combining both religious and psychological counseling. He showed her a sketch of the girl and her vitals, offering her a folder of copies to post in visible spaces.

"My long-term residents have been with me for a while," Sister Betty told him. "The most recent new resident was last year. I will certainly let you know if any of my girls has any feedback on this information. The street life is a social one; people know each other. I'm hopeful for you. God works on the side of justice."

"I'd like to be able to talk to your other staff, if I might," Sean said.

"Of course," Sister Betty replied. "I'm here all the time; I am a resident. I also have several priests and nuns who are here to host programs: job skills, GED classes, sometimes adoption counseling. One person stays overnight on a rotation basis so I always have backup. And then there is my kitchen and cleaning staff." She swiveled around in her chair and pulled a clipboard from the wall. "I can have my assistant make you a copy. It's names and numbers, where you can reach them. That's probably easier than rounding anyone up now. There are a lot of people coming and going here."

Sean thanked her, obliged. When she returned with photocopies, he looked over the list; there seemed to be nearly as many staff as residents.

"I'm curious," she asked. "Was the victim pregnant?"

"I'm not at liberty to say," he replied. The truth was, the final autopsy would confirm that and wasn't due for a few weeks. "Why do you ask?"

"A lot of our residents over the years have been pregnant. We've successfully overseen over a dozen adoptions in my years here. It's the upside of difficult work."

"That's wonderful," he said. 'I'm glad centers like this exist. You make my workload more manageable."

Sister Betty smiled and showed him out.

● ● ●

Sean arrived back at the precinct midday. He had a stack of people to cold-call, staff of various programs that he had visited in the past few days. Ren was at her desk, doing online research.

"What's the word?" Ren asked him.

"I've been to all twelve programs. No immediate ID, which isn't surprising. But I've got a whole stack of staffers for us to call, and the centers are on the lookout."

Sean handed Ren call sheets from the programs he'd been to. She looked them over. They were lists of support staff that worked with homeless youth all over the city.

"We're going to need to focus on calling these people,"

Sean said. "They're more likely to have seen something than the program directors, I would imagine. I talked to Sid on the way in. He said there is nothing new from the tip line."

Ren wasn't listening to him. She was looking over one of the sheets Sean had just given her, tapping her pencil. "This is weird," she said.

"What's that?" Sean asked.

"There is a guy on staff at Westside. His name is familiar."

"An old beau of yours?"

Ren shot him a look, then smiled. She pulled out a folder from her desk, opened it, and scanned it until she found what she was looking for.

"Yup. Strange," she said.

"How long are you going to leave me in the dark?"

"One of the staff at Westside has the same name as a man on the Air Canada flight manifest."

"Let me guess," Sean said. "Michael Smith."

Ren shot him another look. They were both tired and punchy. Then she asked him: "How many David Skardas do you know?"

CHAPTER SEVEN

Lydia Merton swam her final lap, the water undulating out from her in small, ladylike waves. She was graceful in the water, a swan. When she reached the pool's edge, she pulled herself up, rubbing a towel through her hair and another around her body. It was mid-afternoon. She loved the splendid isolation. Most of the other hotel patrons were business people and tourists, rushing off to start their days well before Lydia was fully roused.

She had been at the hotel a week and had already settled into a routine: she woke at eight, got an Americano from the Tully's in the lobby, and enjoyed it along with a complimentary copy of *USA Today* that was delivered to her door each morning. She ate a handful of raw almonds and a carton of Trader Joe's yogurt, which she fit snugly into the minibar alongside the rack of tiny gin bottles and overpriced M&Ms. Sometimes she turned on CNN for more news. On days when she had class, she showered and got ready. Other days she swam laps, sometimes luxuriating in the hot tub for a few minutes afterward.

As it turned out, life at the University Best Western wasn't too bad. The police had brought her suitcase and laptop, plus a Hefty bag full of requested items. The only real challenge was the food. Breakfast was the only meal she could scratch together at the hotel. She was getting tired of all the meals out. Otherwise, though, she was adjusting. It was a bit, she supposed, like being a visiting professor somewhere.

Today when she returned to her room, she noticed the red light on her bedside phone flashing. She ignored it, getting into the shower and lingering under the spray. By the time she was out, swaddled in terry cloth, she was ravenous. She ripped open a bag of trail mix, licking salt off her fingers as she ate. She pulled out the dryer and began to style her hair.

At first the dryer drowned out the sound, but after a moment she heard an insistent knocking on her door. She cast a glance at herself in the mirror. She caught an image of the red light flashing on the bedside phone. She walked over to the door and looked through the peephole. A funhouse image, bathed in yellow light, peered back at her. She inhaled deeply and opened the door.

"This couldn't have waited until my office hours?"

Jakob smirked at her. He was a lean, redheaded hipster who often wore T-shirts endorsing some long forgotten trend. Today it was an orange Atari shirt. "I can't believe the news I'm reading," he said. "Did you kill that girl?"

Lydia shooed him inside. "You really think that's funny? Joking about a murder that happened in my house? This room may be under surveillance for all I know."

He pulled open the minibar and examined the contents. "I'm surprised there is anything left in here. Who can resist the seven-dollar scotch with what's on your plate?"

"Nothing is on my plate, Jakob. A woman was killed in my house. I had nothing to do with it."

"But you do realize the odds are against you, don't you?"

Lydia said nothing.

"Most homicides are committed by someone who knew the victim. The police are anxious to close this case. The D.A. is looking ahead to the next election."

"Yes, but I didn't know this girl, Jakob. The police believe me."

"You don't really trust what those detectives are telling

you, do you? Every sap sitting on death row made that fatal mistake."

She opened her mouth to speak, but found that she had nothing to say. The truth was, she was starting to have nightmares about going to prison.

Lydia dismissed the dark thoughts from her mind. She walked over to Jakob and closed the minibar. She took his face in her hands and kissed him.

An hour later, the red light on the nightstand phone was still flashing. Lydia got up and examined herself in the mirror. Her hair was a mess of tangles. She needed to shower again. She sat down on the bed and hit the replay button. There were three messages left about an hour apart that morning, all saying pretty much the same thing. She listened with intent to the third:

"Ms. Merton, this is Detective Ren Copeland from the Seattle East precinct calling you again. I left you a few messages this morning. Not sure if you got them. Anyway, just wanted to let you know that it is standard procedure in an investigation like this to look at a person's phone records. I've got a copy of your landline records here in front of me, including your calls to 911. Then there is your cell phone. I'd like to ask you about a couple of texts you made on the day you returned to Seattle. I'd like to state that you are not under any suspicion. It's just my job to connect all the dots and eliminate any loose ends."

Lydia sat on the bed, listening to Detective Copeland's voice. She was thinking of that last morning at the Deer Lodge. David had gotten up early to hike the Lake Louise trail one last time. When he got back they had ordered room service: waffles with maple butter, smoked bacon, and orange juice so fresh it made her eyes water.

When they left the lodge that morning, a small sliver moon was still in the sky, with a bright star beside it. Lydia stood in the cold October morning, shivering, waiting for David to pull the rental car around front. She had gathered her sweater around her, closed her eyes, and made a wish.

Later, it had occurred to her that what she had seen in the sky that morning was probably too bright and persistent to be a star. It was probably a planet. And no one ever wished upon a planet.

It was a curious fact, though: since she had returned, her wish was coming true.

• • •

"You've never heard of Harlot's Web?" Ramon asked, incredulous. He reached for a cocktail shaker and emptied the rest of the drink into Ren's martini glass. She drank it greedily. Lime sorbet and liquor slid down her throat, numbing her blissfully. She reached for the platter in front of her and popped a gougère in her mouth. Savory cheese pastry with chunks of sea salt melted on her tongue. This would mean an extra mile of running in the morning, but it was worth it.

"They opened for Sparklehorse at the Paramount. Didn't Bebe tell you about that show?" Ramon was often mystified by his sister's lack of musical knowledge, but his comment tonight had an edge. Ren sensed what was coming next. "We want to set you up with their drummer."

Ramon rarely left a social encounter without making new friends, so his encounter with the band was hardly surprising. He was the type to chat up people outside of men's rooms and waiting in line. He was perfect for his job for the same reason he could never be a detective: he trusted people until they gave him reason not to. While Ren hadn't had a close friend since prep school, her brother would have to rent out a stadium for his funeral.

Ren took another sip of her drink. "Dear brother, I am in

the midst of a homicide case. I'm about to gain back a pound from your buttery pastry and have no way to work it off. Do you think I have time for a date?"

They were at Sanctuary, Ramon's business in Pioneer Square. Its walls were painted a lustrous Tuscan red, which contrasted dramatically with the black tile floors. Religious iconography filled the interior: In addition to a mosaic of the Virgin of Guadalupe on the west wall, there was an oak confessional in one corner, a jukebox that played spirituals and hymns, and tableau featuring rosary beads and votive candles. Even the coasters were prayer cards. Ren's cocktail glass was currently resting on Mary Magdalene.

"You've got to try this," Bebe said, emerging from behind a velvet curtain. She placed a pie tin on the bar. It was filled with a pastry dusted with powdered sugar. Ren took a fork and pulled off the shell. Steam rose, with the aroma of nutmeg and spicy lamb. She took a bite.

"It's fantastic, isn't it?" Bebe poured some cassis into a champagne flute and then topped it with prosecco. She took a sip. "I told your brother he didn't need to go to Provence to learn to cook. He could have just paid more attention to me growing up."

Ren took one more bite of the lamb dish before handing the fork to her brother. "Please cut me off. I've already got to do six miles tomorrow."

Ramon dunked the fork and the cocktail shaker into a sink of sudsy water. There were three of them up and down the bar, hidden from view. "I just told Ren about our setup idea. She doesn't seem interested. She hasn't even heard of Harlot's Web."

"Why are you surprised?" Bebe said. "Your sister has been to maybe five live shows in her life." She paused dramatically. "And one of them was Britney Spears."

Bebe had been beautiful once, but now she had a slightly haggard air about her, like a house in need of a paint job. Her hair was untamed frizz, and her eyes were set deep into her face like black sand pearls. She had had more boyfriends than there were stars on Old Glory. And there was nothing she loved as much as her kids.

Neither Ramon nor Bebe had a great track record with relationships, but they remained starry-eyed romantics on the inevitability of true love. They had tried to set up Ren a few times over the years, but she was skilled at ducking out. Ren didn't date much. She wasn't even sure how to do it.

"I've got one more thing for you to try before I cut you loose," Ramon said, proffering a small plate and fork. "I'm going to call this Quiche Bebe."

Their mother beamed and skittered off behind the velvet curtain.

Ren knew that protest was futile. She took a bite. The quiche had the consistency of a soufflé. She could taste savory bacon and hints of chives. She let out a moan.

"The secret is the crust," Ramon said. "It's croissant dough."

"It's official," Ren said. "Anyone who frequents Sanctuary from now on will end up a fat alcoholic. I mean that in the best possible sense." She fished her phone out of her purse and checked for messages. "I wish I could get Sean to come here. He would love this food."

"Yeah, what's up with that? Is he antisocial or something? I haven't seen him since last Thanksgiving. He was dating that woman. What was her name?"

"Lindsay," Ren said.

"Right. Are they still together?"

"I'm not sure. He doesn't talk too much about her anymore."

Ren pulled her coat on. "Brother, this food is fabulous. I

think you will more than earn back the cost of the trip." She reached over the bar and kissed him on the cheek.

"Don't be such a stranger," he said. "I want to see you before Thanksgiving."

Ren promised him he would and then darted behind the velvet curtain to say good-bye to their mother.

• • •

It was pitch black as Ren parked her Camaro near the Eastlake docks. She lived in the first quay. She had purchased the houseboat eight years ago with money left to her by her grandfather. He was a nightclub owner for fifty years who had died owning some prime Seattle real estate. Ren had just enough to buy her place.

A railway track separated the dock from the land, a remnant of distant mining days. She checked her mailbox, which was empty save for a few flyers. She made her way down the wooden steps.

Colored paper lanterns streamed up and down the dock, creating the feeling of enchantment. Flowerboxes stood on some front railings, Nepalese peace flags on others. The pathway between houseboats was well lit, but it didn't matter much: Ren lived in the first on the right. On its top, smoke churned out of a striped stovepipe.

Ren stopped cold, watching the plume of gray smoke rise. Someone was on her houseboat. They had built a fire. Ren didn't have her gun on her. She had left it at home when she stopped back after work. She thought for a moment, and then she remembered the knife and handcuffs she kept in the glove compartment of her car. She ran down the dock and up the stairs to the parking lot. The knife was where she left it.

As she opened her front door, she heard the flutter of wings and got a blast of warmth from the fire.

"Come out with your hands up!" she bellowed into the empty space. She moved through the living room, checking the loft and the bathroom. No one was there.

Her cat, Ariel, was lounging on the couch. Puck, the parrot, was safe in his cage. They seemed undisturbed.

Ren took a seat. She was feeling a little tipsy from the cocktail. Was it possible she had started a fire earlier that evening and forgotten about it? She didn't think it was. But the only other option was harder to imagine. Only one other person had a key to the houseboat. Ren hadn't seen her for years.

CHAPTER EIGHT

When Ren awoke, the houseboat was quiet. Lake Union was still, the fire in the potbellied stove had burned down to a few embers, and Puck was asleep in his birdcage. There was a warm spot on the duvet where Ariel had been. Ren rolled over before forcing herself to get up. It was dark out.

The memory of the previous night, and the feeling that someone might have been on the houseboat, had stayed with her. She was feeling better about it now that morning was here.

Ren pulled on a pair of running pants and a T-shirt, then a Gore-Tex jacket. She searched for her shoes, which she found near the vent in the bathroom. Ariel had migrated to the warmth there. Ren pulled on socks and stroked the cat a few times.

Her houseboat was tiny, but she loved it. She slept in a loft up a set of stairs with a view of the western part of the lake. Her bed was under a skylight, so she fell asleep under starlight some nights. She had a camper-sized kitchen and a standup shower in the back of the first floor. In her living room, a couch and a wooden armchair faced a potbellied stove. She kept her laptop on her coffee table and used it for Netflix and other streaming media. In one corner near the front door was Puck's birdcage. In the other was a gilded Buddha from Phnom Penh that Ramon had given her. Ren had draped some beads over it. She kept a few photos and mementos on this altar. It had been four years since she had meditated before it.

There was frost on the railroad tracks as she exited the quay. She hoped the sidewalks wouldn't be slippery. She had just over an hour to run six miles, and she didn't want to be slowed down.

The first mile was always the worst. She had taught herself to run by repeating a mantra: *Turn back after mile one.* It was a trick to get her going because nothing was ever as bad as the first mile. After that she had the endorphins to motivate her. Sometimes they hit in the last mile, as she returned downhill from Interlaken Park; sometimes they hit when she was at home under the hot shower spray. The promise of these were what kept her moving.

Every other morning, for her entire adult life, this is what Ren did. She ran and ran and ran—past the Lenin statue in Fremont and the Troll under Aurora Bridge, up alongside the coffeehouses on Capitol Hill, and through the wooded trails in Montlake.

Today, the girl was on her mind as she ran. Ren had been having strange dreams since the case began. The image of the young woman on the floor of Lydia's TV room, starring up at the ceiling, gave way to strange hallucinatory images. Last night she had dreamt she was in a swampy wooded area, stepping over roots that looked like snakes. She looked up at a large oak tree dripping with Spanish moss. She saw a woman hanging from ropey vines near the branches. When she got more closely she saw that the woman was Lydia Merton.

Ren paid no heed to premonitions. She didn't believe in psychic messages or help from beyond the grave. If such things happened, more homicides would be solved. The fact of the matter was that most crimes of this nature were hard to settle. The girl may have had an abusive boyfriend with her at the house. It was possible that she was a drug dealer or a prostitute. The detail that nagged at Ren was the location where she had been killed. Why was she in Lydia Merton's house?

By the time Ren got back to Eastlake, her body was

aching. She stood at the top of the stairs leading to the quay and stretched. It was a curiosity to her that running made her upper body ache.

When she got inside her house, she pulled the chip out of her shoe. She had burned five hundred fifty calories. When she stepped on the scale after her shower, there would be no surprises. She would weigh one hundred forty-five pounds, as she did most days.

The scale hadn't shifted much in fourteen years. Ren viewed the number as a type of job security. There was no official law against obese detectives, but it was also rare you saw one. Some rules are as constant as they are unspoken. Ren wasn't fooling herself. Since buying the houseboat eight years ago, she had no savings. Over half her paycheck went to her mortgage. She got her books from the library and never traveled. The money simply wasn't there at the end of each month. Ren needed her job and she needed her pension. Staying fit increased the odds.

Just out of the shower, Ren was feeling pretty good. The coffee percolated, a mixture of three Peet's blends that she kept in her freezer. The aroma filled the air as she dried her hair and fed Ariel and Puck. She poured herself a mug of coffee, added some half and half, and made herself some instant oatmeal. She removed three clementines from a tower on her kitchen table and ate them as she drank her morning cup.

The first few hours of Ren's day were a strange netherworld where food had little grip over her. She had to push herself some days to finish her oatmeal. Often this world tilted on its axis by noon. She craved food like an ex-smoker does nicotine: sesame bagels with cream cheese, thick chunks of milk chocolate, brioche with pearl sugar. At quitting time it was tart margaritas and nachos with sour cream.

Ren had another mantra for those moments. She repeated

it, sometimes aloud, when she couldn't stand it anymore: *Wait Until Sunday*. Once a week, she allowed herself to eat anything she wanted. She could go to Saul's Deli for eggs benedict or stop by Luisa's for veal piccata. The promise of another splurge day on the horizon kept her going.

Ren arrived at the Seattle East precinct around nine. This was her usual schedule. She parked in her reserved spot and took the stairs to the fourth floor. Her desk was near a large window with a view of downtown. She could see the Space Needle and, on a clear day, the snow-capped Olympic range.

"Hey, Ren, we're placing bets. You in?" Sid Hopkins loped over from his desk at the other side of the room. He was in his usual getup: slip-on Chinese shoes and a corduroy jacket. Behind his ear, he kept an unlit cigarette, the way others would a sharpened pencil. He had a manila envelope in his hand. "I've got a hundred on Conlin, Jason has the same on Wu, and Jasper in the crime lab is betting on Sean. Don't tell him."

Ren had no money for a wager, and she wouldn't place a bet even if she had. The precinct had a gossip tree that rivaled a redwood.

"Here's another wager," she said to him. "When I have a baby, who *won't* be the father?" Sid took the jab and slunk away, his short dreadlocks bopping in time to his movements.

As she powered up her computer, Ren noticed a Post-It stuck to her chair. It was Sean's handwriting.

Meet me in I A.

She understood his shorthand. Ren walked to the interview room, nodding a silent greeting to Jason Twick as she passed him. Jason had been doing a thorough job with the secondary leads on the case, and she appreciated the assistance.

Ren opened the door to the interview room to find her partner standing over a table full of evidence bags. The lights were off, and a slide projector showed images on the wall.

"What's all this?" Ren asked.

"Seattle Main brought this over this morning. It's evidence from a suicide that they're now classifying as suspicious. They think it might be connected to our case."

Ren grabbed a set of latex gloves and snapped them on.

"Young guy found shot in the temple near the ferries to Vashon. They haven't been able to ID him, but look at this." He held up a Ziploc bag. Ren hit the overhead lights to get a better view. It was a Washington State ID for a woman named Cedar Heekin with an address near Sea-Tac airport. She had long strawberry blonde hair. Her age was listed at eighteen. It surprised Ren; the girl in the photos had the weathered look of someone years older. She had noticed this quality before in people at the margins. Hardship added years.

"This could be our girl," Ren said. "Her ID was found on him?"

"It was found in his jacket pocket. But no wallet on him or ID."

"He's got her ID but not his?" Ren hit the lights again and looked more intently at the crime scene photos projected on the wall. "This is where they found him?" She was looking at images of a homeless shantytown under an overpass. In the distance, there was a ferry port. "Any witnesses?"

"They weren't able to get any on record, other than the homeless guy who found the body. Originally they thought the kid had gone down there at night and shot himself, but the medical examiner thinks the bullet may have been from too far away to be self-inflicted."

"So someone killed him just a few hundred feet from the bay?" Ren said. "Why wouldn't they dump him in the water?"

"Maybe the person disposing the body was interrupted. Had to do it quickly for fear of getting caught?"

"We should check out the address on this ID," Ren said.

"We might be able to get the girl's body claimed. We don't know anything about the identity of the boy?"

"Not yet. We have the clothes he was found in, and that's about it."

Ren picked up a few bags and had a look. She hit the overheads again. The kid had been found wearing jeans and a heavy jean jacket. His T-shirt was stained with his blood. She was looking at it now. The red and orange ran together, creating a tie-dye effect. There was a white logo on the front of the shirt, also stained with blood.

"Atari," Ren said, reading the logo. "Remember that?"

CHAPTER NINE

Nola Vance had worked for the Seattle East precinct for five years, ever since the day she had tired of bartending and scanned Craigslist for the nearest path of escape. Her only radical act since that day was marrying her longtime boyfriend. After eight years of polyamory, Nola was tired of shocking people with her stories. She had done everything under the sun, and she found that she liked doing it best with Harris. So they married. They lived in an apartment on Olive Way, where they ate panini and homemade gelato and occasionally a cake shaped like a Gothic cathedral. This was another benefit of marriage: they had received most of their Williams-Sonoma gift registry.

Camille Roemer and Nola Vance had the kind of relationship that made coming to work a pleasure. They went to lunch at Octo Sushi a few times a month, talking about their weekends over swamp rolls and green tea. Camille had gone to Nola's wedding, held in the Chinese Botanical Gardens one summer. She was in the wedding photos, standing astride a large jade dragon.

Nola liked Camille. In slow periods, she let her read books at her desk, so long as she looked busy if anyone stopped by. Nola had read *The Shining* and *The Witching Hour* on company time.

All of this changed when Joshua Conlin took over. He was a small, serpentine man with a bump on his head and a blond ponytail trailing down his back. He dressed in tweed and ate hard-boiled eggs for lunch. When Nola's birthday came around, he balked at expensing her pho from Tangerine Tree.

Nola despised the guy. If she had been asked to draw up a list of the top five most loathsome people she'd ever known, Joshua Conlin would be number two. She couldn't wait for him to be banished back to the third floor where he belonged.

So Nola did what any reasonable person would do when faced with a prick boss. She snooped.

It started when he would leave his computer on while he went out for a bit. Nola would wait a few moments, enough time for him to leave the building. Sometimes she peered out the window until she spotted his stick figure sauntering down Pine Street. Then she would sneak into his office.

She learned from his browser history that he had an account at the dating site cupidandpsyche.com. In his photos he hid the bump on his head under a hat. His interests included insect collecting and tango. He said he wouldn't date a woman who was even slightly overweight.

Other days Nola went through his desk. He kept meticulous files, color-coded. There were printouts of email exchanges between himself and the HR director, a plump woman named DeDe Damen who seemed to have a crush on him. She had written up Detective Lukela for tardiness and Henry Wu for abusing his phone privileges, both at Conlin's suggestion.

There was also a series of email printouts between Conlin and DeDe that Nola couldn't quite make sense of. They were titled "Christmas '10" and went back and forth for a period of days. Nola couldn't find the original email. The last missive was from HR. It said this:

I refer you to section 9.08 of the Code: "If any person violates the principles of ethics or discretion, as stipulated in the handbook, he or she may face termination."

Nola had deduced that the subject of the emails was the previous year's company Christmas party. It had been held at a supper club in Bellevue. Nola remembered that night. She had rented a flapper dress and gotten drunk on pink ladies. She and Harris had jitterbugged the night away; he was late the next morning for his shift at the Coffee Messiah.

Something had happened that night, and Conlin seemed to think it violated the ethics code. He seemed bent on getting someone fired.

The day before Camille came back from maternity leave, Nola helped Conlin empty out the office. She opened the windows wide, ridding the fifth floor of his tweedy stench. She took his box of files, with the HR emails, down to the third floor, depositing them on his desk with a flourish.

But she never told anyone what she had seen in those emails, not even her husband.

• • •

Bridge Heekin lived in a house the color of black tar near the airport. Planes flew overhead day and night, so close that he could sometimes see the Inuit logo headed for Anchorage. There were days he wanted to climb aboard and get lost on the frozen tundra.

The day that the detectives came, Bridge had just fed his yellow boa a butterscotch-colored guinea pig. It was lodged in his throat, being digested slowly, when the doorbell rang. Tits looked sideways, tiny pig feet sticking out of his mouth like pitchforks. "It's just the cops," Bridge said to the snake. He had been expecting them.

He noticed the girl cop first. He resisted the desire to pull off his shirt and show her the inked Polynesian in a grass skirt just above his shoulder blade. It wasn't every day you met someone who looked like your tattoo.

He showed the detectives in, gesturing for them to sit on the yellow couch. In the background, Judge Judy scolded a teenager for stealing a friend's car. The volume was low, but he could still hear her big mouth.

"I know why you're here," Bridge said. "My stepdaughter is the one in the news, isn't she?"

"We don't know that for sure," Ren said. "You haven't tried to ID the body yet...."

Bridge shook his head. The truth was, he might like to scatter Cedar's ashes on Elliott Bay, sprinkle them over the water like fish food. Or maybe he'd take them to Rainier and bury them on the trail where Blue was. "I've been depressed since my wife died. I don't get out much. I wasn't completely sure until I saw you walk up just now."

This was only partially true. In his youth, Bridge had served eighteen months at Walla Walla for assault. He and Cedar fought like cats and dogs, a fact the detectives would surely learn if they started nosing around. He wasn't about to do them any favors framing him up for Cedar's death.

Ren gave the house a once-over. The living room was bare, except for a TV that was encased in a wood console, as if trying to class up the joint. She could see into the kitchen, which had wallpaper that was an impossibly sunny yellow. On the counter there were two dozen prescription pill bottles. Either Bridge had health problems, or he hadn't cleared things away since his wife died.

"We'd like to know more about Cedar," Ren said. "I assume you've been following the news. Do you have any idea what she was doing in that house when she died?"

Bridge scratched his head. "My wife died last spring. She'd been sick for a while. Cedar and me never got along, but after Blue passed we just couldn't be in the same room together. Cedar started staying away more and more. The news keeps saying she's homeless, but I don't think that's right. She had her ways."

"You don't know of any connection between Cedar and a woman named Lydia Merton?"

Bridge shook his head.

"Did Cedar have a boyfriend? Anyone she introduced you to?"

"I think she had plenty," Bridge said. "But I never met them."

Ren was a bit nonplussed by this encounter. How could a man be so detached from his child's death? Was it really blood that bound people? Or was it possible to be so depressed that another person's death was just a passing observation?

"We'd like to have a look at Cedar's room," she declared, and Bridge nodded. He took them up a short set of carpeted stairs to the second floor. Cedar's room was the first on the right. A single bed was still made up, flanked by posters of unicorns on the walls and a bookshelf filled with fantasy novels. Her CD rack was mostly hippie music. Ren recognized a lot of the titles from her mother's vinyl collection. Cedar and Bebe could have talked music. On the bookshelf there was a snow globe from Chinatown in San Francisco, and a small gold box filled with concert ticket stubs.

Ren spotted a Greyhound bus stub amidst the concert tickets and pulled it out. It appeared that Cedar had traveled to California the previous spring.

"Do you know anything about this trip she took?" Ren asked, holding the ticket up in the light. It was from Seattle to San Francisco in March of the previous spring.

Bridge glanced at it. "After Blue died, Cedar wanted to see the town where she was born. I gave her the money to do it."

"She was born near San Francisco?" Ren asked.

Bridge nodded. "I think so. I don't really know. I'm not

sure she even went to the town where she was born. I think she just wanted an excuse to meet a bunch of fruits and nuts in Frisco."

The detectives gave Bridge their cards as well as information about how he could claim Cedar's body. They took the name of the high school Cedar had last attended. They would send a team to canvass it as soon as possible.

Bridge thought about this encounter later, as he was eating his Hungry Man in the kitchen. He was remembering his wedding day. Blue wore a lace dress and platform boots. They had marshmallow frosting on their cake and danced cheek to cheek. Cedar had scowled every time the photographer tried to get her to pose. Bridge wanted to backhand her for acting out at her mother's wedding, but he wouldn't do that to Blue. She loved her daughter. Plus he knew what happened to men who hit minors. He wasn't going back to Walla Walla. Bridge would snort Pepsi out of his nose to anyone claiming that prison doesn't scare a man straight. It had certainly scared him.

Bridge missed Blue every day. He could feel her presence on the steps as he walked downstairs in the morning, and in a blast of cold wind as he worked in the yard. He thought of his own mother, a flaming redhead who had married seven times. She had an expression: *You know where you can find sorry in my house? In the dictionary, between shit and syphilis.*

Maybe this was why he didn't feel much sorrow that Cedar was dead. He couldn't bring himself to care about bringing his stepdaughter's killer to justice, like those families on Court TV. He dumped the detectives' cards in the trash along with his Hungry Man box.

Bridge had a persistent thought, though, in the days after the detectives' visit. It struck him from time to time, much like the memory of his wife. It went something like this: *There are people in life who are worth killing. Cedar wasn't one of them.*

• • •

They had just passed the Starbucks tower when Sean asked, "Did you know that mermaid is twenty feet high?" He was referencing the corporate offices of the coffee chain, which were to the left as they drove. He held his hand up to the sky, capturing the logo between his thumb and index finger. "From here I can scale her down to half an inch."

When Ren said nothing, he said, "She looks like a contortionist. You ever notice that?"

Ren took an exit toward downtown.

"You see that boa in Bridge's house?" Sean asked. "It was snacking on a rat like it was a Hostess Twinkie."

Ren said nothing.

"You didn't catch that, Ren?"

She had, but she was in no mood for Sean's jocularity just now. Not that she didn't understand it: they were buzzing from the information they had gotten today. That suicide under the bridge had been their lucky break.

"My mind was on bigger issues than snakes," Ren said. "It's not every day you encounter a guy who just hasn't gotten around to ID'ing his dead stepdaughter."

"I know," Sean said, getting serious. He knew how to snap back at just the right moment. "It's not hard to see why she left. That house felt like a mausoleum."

"So, where we headed now?" he asked, looking at the unfamiliar terrain. He hadn't been down this way since the last time he went shopping.

"I've been thinking about a couple things. I want to make a stop."

Years ago Ren had worked as a beat cop in this neighborhood. The commercial district brought out shoplifters and pickpockets. A few blocks down there were petty drug deals and prostitutes. South of the commercial district was Pioneer

Square and beyond that ferries to Vashon Island. This was where the boy had been found shot.

Ren pulled into Ramon's reserved commercial spot at Sanctuary. He didn't open the bar until four, so they had a good ninety minutes to make use of his parking space before he showed up. The shantytown beneath the bridge was a few blocks from the bar.

"My brother wants to know why you're such a stranger these days," Ren said as they began the brisk walk from Pioneer Square. Sean had been known to hang out at the bar in the past. He and Ramon were kindred spirits.

"It's that new Virgin on the wall," Sean said. "Have you ever looked at her? I swear she's gangland."

Ren laughed. Ramon had found the piece at a church auction the previous spring. It was a mosaic made of colored glass from a church in Echo Park.

They walked the rest of the way in silence, a bitter wind coming in from the bay, until they reached the shantytown, a small village made of shopping carts and cardboard boxes. It reeked of astringent urine. The ground was littered with fruit peels and discarded litter. Ren had to resist the impulse to cover her mouth and nose with a handkerchief. She didn't want to appear disrespectful.

A man, dressed in a Grinnell sweatshirt and wearing a large, tweed overcoat, sat on an old mattress. Near him was an acoustic guitar case bulging with clothes and a stack of paperback novels. "A fair lady visits," he said aloud, without looking up. "What do you think about that, Hen?"

Ren looked around to see whom he was addressing. Just behind him, there was a copper-colored chicken resting on the mattress.

"That's my compatriot, Henny," the man said to Ren. "Bought her in the International District on what can understatedly be termed her lucky day. Care to spare a shekel for some feed?"

Ren reached into her wallet and pulled out a five. He took it and then produced a handful of chicken feed from his coat pocket. Henny waddled to the foreground and pecked away.

"What's that you say, Henny?" the man said, leaning his ear closer to the fowl. "These people are here about the boy that died? Why do you say that?"

"That's a smart bird you've got there," Ren said. "Were you here the day they found the body?"

"Can't say that I was," the man said. "We all had beds that night, at a Temple in the North End. But a fellow traveler found a gun in these parts and was that much richer for it."

"He found a gun here and sold it?"

"Yes, to a pawn shop. He didn't say which one."

Sean gave Ren an incredulous look, imploring her to wrap this errand up.

"I have another question for you," Ren said. "Do you know someone who goes by the name the Duchess?"

The homeless man looked in the distance, as if recalling something. Then he said: "In her day, the Duchess stopped a block. Her father owned half of Capitol Hill, or so the story goes. But a glass pipe brings us all under the bridge eventually."

"That's right," Ren said. "Have you seen her around recently?"

The man shook his head. He had stopped speaking. Ren reached into her pocket and handed him a twenty.

"Do you have a message for the Duchess if I see her?" he asked, pulling Henny into his lap. He stroked behind her ears as she clucked.

Ren thought of all the things she might say, a flood of words: about the years she'd lost pining for her, about how the betrayal shaped her into the woman she was now, about how she'd never love again because of the one she loved first.

"Tell her to stay off my boat," Ren said and walked away.

• • •

That night on the houseboat, Ren couldn't shake a feeling. It followed her from room to room and occupied more space in her brain than the attention she was giving the case. She shut down her computer and dialed a number.

Hattie Mott answered on the first ring. She was an investigator that Ren sometimes used when she wanted to keep things on the down low. Hattie owed her a few. Ren was calling this one in.

"I'd like you to research a classmate of mine from St. Veronica Preparatory. Her name was Delphine Hutching." She spelled it for her. "We graduated together in 1996. The last I saw her she was living on the streets. She's a meth addict, at least some of the time."

"Addicts are often hard to track down," Hattie said. "They fall off the grid."

"Her parents won't be hard to find. Her father owns Milton Brothers, the toy company. See if you can find out anything. I just need the basics, like where I can find her if I need to."

Hattie took down a few more details and promised to be in touch soon. Ren was grateful. She had enough on her plate without chasing down an old ghost.

Ren sat until the darkness wrapped itself around her. She was remembering their last week at Veronica Prep. They were flush with the fever that hits at the point of no return: their lives as students were over; the parental chains had fallen to the ground. She had no way of knowing it at the time, but Ren would never again feel that same kind of abandon.

Del's graduation party had been on a yacht. They snuck

into the master suite, Ren in a sea-foam green dress, and had sex on the bed. Ren could still feel Del's hand in hers as they stood at the stern, looking at the Seattle skyline, all lit up in blue and white. *The Duchess* was the name of the yacht, after Del's mother, who had killed herself when Delphine was two.

Ren pictured Del at seventeen: her rock-star physique, with the rail-thin body and shaggy, unkempt hair, a crucifix dangling off her body in a way that let everyone on campus know she was only there for show. Del had made the young hearts of Veronica Prep leap when she entered a room. Ren's was one of them.

Delphine Hutching, Ren thought, scarcely believing that she was back. *Why are you coming around again?*

CHAPTER TEN

"The basic message is that God is so great that he can forgive anything."

Lydia nodded her head, impressed. A student, Pippa, had just summed up the main theme of Endo's *Silence*. There was a student like this every quarter, one that wasn't sidetracked by the poetry and gore of this novel and could see its simple theological message.

Lydia's Intro to Global Religious Traditions combined study of each of the major religions with a short work that encapsulated the spirit of its theology. For Judaism, it was Potok's *The Chosen;* for Buddhism, Hesse's *Siddhartha*. This week they were focused on Christianity.

"So what's the point of morality, anyhow?" Pippa said. She was dressed in a blue silk Chinese coat. A porcelain chopstick held her unruly hair in place. "If God will forgive anything, why be moral?"

Lydia surveyed the class. "What do you think? Why be moral?"

A few hands shot up, talking about the beloved community and the chosen tribes. Lydia was gratified: some students were getting the main themes of the course. This was the kind of debate students got lively in, mostly because they could engage in it without having done the reading. Jakob usually was active at moments like this, but he was absent from class today. It was just as well. Lydia was tired of dealing with him.

"Virtue is its own reward," one student offered. "You can gain self-esteem by doing good in the world."

"I think it's all pointless," Pippa said. "Theism is the sucker's bet."

Lydia let the conversation trail on for a bit, holding back, before offering her own take on the value of religion. She talked about the regeneration that comes from spirituality, and she offered examples of people and communities lifted up by some numinous spiritual force.

Lydia's own journey to faith had been perilous, complicated as it was by the devastation of losing her parents when she was just out of college. They had died within six months of each other. At her mother's funeral, the officiating priest had talked about young children he had seen die and how the length of years were not guaranteed. What was important was the relationship one had with God, in the end. Lydia still seethed when she thought of that insensitive eulogy. How disrespectful to her dear mother, who had suffered cancer for eighteen months, ending up yellow and lifeless. The memory still made Lydia ache.

A few months after her father died, the parish had assigned a priest to look in on Lydia. She was a young woman who had lost both of her parents within six months: her mother to cancer, her father to a brain hemorrhage. David visited a few times to see how she was doing and then called her to see why she wasn't attending mass. He didn't push her to attend but seemed genuinely concerned for her. They had long conversations that eventually turned into lunches and dinners. They liked to cook and drink wine and discuss theology. After a few years, they fell in love.

In David, Lydia saw someone devoted to a life of service, driven by a belief that human agency determines the state of the world. Left to the craven desires that are inherent in humans, the world was the Devil's playground. Lydia was amazed by the devotion David showed to the Church, even when they asked him to deny his love for her. He was a man of principle, born at the wrong time. If the day came when Rome reversed its position on celibacy, they would be free to marry. Lydia fancied that their lives were not unlike the experiences of gay and lesbian couples in bygone eras.

Lydia wrapped up the hour and walked back to her office. It was three o'clock, but already she could feel the winter darkness on its way. It was chilly as she crossed campus. She thought of the assortment of teas she had in her office desk drawer. Maybe half a chocolate bar as well. She had office hours scheduled today until four thirty but she didn't expect to see many students.

As she approached her office, Lydia saw someone on the floor, blocking her door. It was a peculiar sight: Someone was sitting in the doorframe, using it as a brace. It was a girl, with short, cropped brown hair. On her feet she wore black espadrilles, laced up her leg with rainbow ribbons. They reminded Lydia of a maypole.

"May I help you?"

"Dr. Merton?"

This happened often. Students didn't know the difference between a professor and an instructor. "I'm Lydia Merton."

"Do you remember me?" the girl asked.

Lydia had never seen her before, or if she had she had forgotten. "No, I'm sorry."

"I was in your summer session last year. Ruby West."

Lydia looked closer. The young woman had olive skin and hazel eyes. Her teeth were slightly crooked.

"Oh, yes. I do remember you." She didn't, but it seemed pointless to dwell on that at a moment like this. "How may I help you?" Lydia opened her office, switched on the lights and cleared off space for Ruby to sit. She took a seat opposite her, trying not to think about the bittersweet chocolate bar that was in her desk drawer. It would taste so good with a cup of Earl Grey.

"I was thinking of taking your class next quarter," Ruby said. "And I was looking you up online, and I saw that your degree was from GTU."

Lydia froze. It took her a moment to reply. "No. I have a degree from the Evergreen State College in comparative and alternative religions."

The girl looked at her, her doe eyes wide. "You didn't write a thesis about Shadow Rock?"

"No," Lydia lied. She hoped she was concealing her emotions. Her heart was beating wildly in her chest.

The girl shrugged, looking dejected. "I found this thesis online by someone named Lydia Merton. It was an ethnography about the place where I grew up. Shadow Rock is what they call it. It's kind of a religious commune, if you can understand that concept. I moved away with my dad when I was ten. The author had spent time there, after I left. I got chills when I was looking at the Pacific website a few days later. It seemed like utter synchronicity."

Lydia smiled. She was feeling slightly sick. "That is certainly a strange coincidence," she said. "But I only hold one degree. Didn't have to do a thesis for a BA."

Ruby kept talking. "I was excited. Shadow Rock was a strange place to grow up. Reading this piece was like having a conversation with someone who'd had the same weird dream that I did. And she interviewed my dad. I've always been curious why he left, and I thought she might know. He doesn't like to talk about Shadow Rock."

"Sorry to have disappointed you," Lydia said. "Can I be of any further assistance to you today?"

The girl shook her head. She looked near tears. Lydia

stood up and motioned the way out. She closed the office door firmly behind her.

Later, she felt slightly guilty about the way she behaved. Here this girl was, probably new to the Pacific Northwest, trying to be friendly and make a connection. Lydia had been nearly rude to her. She imagined the girl walking away from the encounter, salty tears spilling over.

But her immediate thought was not about Ruby West. Instead Lydia's mind ran over and over, racing with the same question: *Who put my thesis online?*

● ● ●

Lieutenant Camille Roemer wanted to smoke. She had quit years ago and had never been much more than a social smoker. But moments like this brought it out. She imagined herself inhaling deeply, tar hitting her lungs. She needed gum to quell the craving, or Red Vines. Something to chomp on was the order of the moment. One of Pablo's chew toys might have come in handy. She could have munched Sophie the Giraffe down to calf size.

She had found over the years that there were three stages to a murder investigation. The first was the agitated state, when she found herself fidgety and stressed. The second was the depressed state, when she fought the impulse to stay in bed all day. The third was a euphoric, rock-star state when the case was settled and going to trial. She was strictly in stage one today. She wanted carcinogens or sugar.

Instead she doodled. She pulled out colored markers and drew on a legal pad. She sketched a cartoon image of a church and another of a tree. It was helping her concentrate.

"So what have you got?" she asked her detectives. They were in her office on the fifth floor of the Seattle East precinct. Camille didn't like to sit behind a desk, so the three of them were sitting in cushy chairs, a coffee table between them. "How are these cases shaping up?"

"We've got the girl ID'd. Her stepfather claimed the body yesterday. We've got Lydia and Skarda with airtight alibis. They weren't in Seattle when Cedar was killed," Ren began. "And we've got this kid found dead downtown with Cedar's ID. A homeless guy said someone picked up the gun and sold it. We've traced it to a pawnshop, but it was unregistered. There were no valuable prints. Nothing to link the gun to anyone."

This happened a lot in police work. Valuable time and resources expended only to get nowhere. "And you don't think this was a murder-suicide?" Camille asked. "Kid killed Cedar at the house, then a few days later couldn't live with himself?"

Ren had been puzzling over this for weeks. "I don't think it's the full story. Look at the Merton house," Ren said. "It's a cottage amidst estates. Why did Cedar choose that house to break into? It can't be the only one that was vacant." Ren had looked into it. Lydia's house was appraised at a third the value of her neighbors on either side.

"I think it's because there was less security," Sean said. They'd been having this debate since the case began. "It was an easier property to access. Or maybe this kid she was with knew the house. He seems to be the right age to be one of Lydia's students."

Sean had talked to the registrar at Pacific Community College, to see if any students had dropped out of sight. Unfortunately, the enrollment was considerable, and it wasn't uncommon for students to come and go. The school wasn't helpful. All they could tell him was that no one had been reported missing.

Camille selected a red, felt-tip marker and began drawing the Golden Gate Bridge. "What about Cedar's stepfather? He has a prior for assault."

"He's a strange guy, but I don't see any motive. And why would he dump her body in Lydia Merton's house? It's illogical."

"What did you find when you searched his property?"

"Mostly nothing. The only thing I've booked into evidence was a Greyhound ticket from last spring. Cedar went down to San Francisco. Bridge said that after her mother died, Cedar was curious to see the town she was born in. He paid for her to go down for a few days."

"And what about Cedar's mother? What do we know about her?"

"Not much. She lived in California when Cedar was born, and married Bridge when Cedar was five. She died of some kind chronic cancer. She'd been sick for a long time, it seems."

Camille put down the marker. "Tell me honestly, how close do you think you are?"

Ren and Sean looked at each other.

"Not at all close," Ren said. "We're missing a crucial piece to this. Lydia says she's never seen the girl before and doesn't know any reason she would break in. And yet to understand who killed Cedar, we have to know why she was in that house."

"You don't think there is any chance Lydia is lying to you about knowing her? You've looked at her phone records?"

"Yes, I subpoenaed both her landline and her cell," Ren said. "She doesn't talk to anyone but Skarda, and not that often. I also have his phone records. He has a huge social network, as you might imagine, and he talks to many of them by phone. His records are so vast that I've delegated that duty to Jason."

Camille nodded and got up. She walked to her desk to check her computer and phone. "I think you're both doing an excellent job with this. I'm inclined to think the simple explanation makes the most sense. Cedar and this boy broke into

Lydia's house, got into a fight, he killed her, and then killed himself when he couldn't live with the guilt. Or maybe he feared he was going to get caught. This story has been in the news."

Ren got up, feeling less certain. She had nagging doubts about closing this case. She wasn't satisfied with the conclusions her boss was making.

"You're both free to go," Camille said, phone to her ear. She was checking her messages. "Let me know if anything comes up."

She smiled as the detectives exited the room. Once they had left her smile turned into a frown. She hit replay and listened to the message again:

"Lieutenant Roemer, this is DeDe Damen from HR. A matter has recently come to my attention, and I need to talk to you about it immediately. I'd prefer that we meet in my office, and I think you might prefer that as well. Please call me at your earliest convenience."

CHAPTER ELEVEN

Sister Betty Holland had run the Westside Home for Girls for fifteen years. She lived in a suite near the back entrance of the facility, which meant that she was largely cut off from her Order, which she had joined as a young woman. Truth be told, she preferred it this way. The residents at Westside saw her as an authority figure, not a colleague. The structured distance helped her maintain a certain air of dignity and authority.

As much as she believed in the goodness of God, Sister Betty had mixed feelings about people. She had seen many circles of hell in this line of work. Many of the residents at Westside were runaways, forced to leave horrendous home lives. Some had ended up on the streets due to drug addiction and alcoholism. Some were just plain weak, expecting things to be easy and finding themselves incompetent to stand up to life's challenges. But there was hope, even in the most downtrodden case. Sister Betty lived by that faith.

Once, Sister Betty had dreamed of marriage and children, imagining a life for herself quite unlike the one she had ended up with. She felt no resentment that things had materialized so differently. There was a numinous force in charge of everyone's fate, and people were foolish to think they had any control over it. She had accepted her role in God's plan.

Sister Betty worked every day to lead her girls to Christ. Those who came through her program had often seen the worst of human nature, and it was understandable they lacked faith. They were literally *God forsaken*. Abused and neglected, if they had any religion at all it was a belief that God had afflicted them. Sister Betty worked to show them that the world could be a different place if more people actively channeled God's grace.

Sister Betty had experienced her fair share of sycophants working in this vocation. Journalists wanted to interview her at times, to profile her life of service, but she refused their requests unless she was certain it would help the church. She got letters from prison inmates, praising her for pages before asking for her help in their appeal. She had even once been offered a backstage pass for a U2 concert. Bono had read about her work and wanted to meet her when the band was passing through town, or so she was told.

Sister Betty had no time for such foolishness. She had learned long ago that admiration was just another type of guilt. The people who wanted to meet her were looking to be absolved. If they could see her as a saint, it would release them of ever feeling more than a passing need to give up the material world. Sister Betty wasn't willing to play along with their delusions. She responded to most requests with a form letter and a brochure about committing to a life in Christ.

As December approached, the Westside Home for Girls was gearing up to host a month of short-term guests. Homeless people would line up outside at five o'clock each night and would be offered dinner and a cot, along with breakfast and a bag lunch the next morning. Sister Betty had hosted these events before, and they were often stressful. The homeless people often reeked of alcohol and human stench. There were always a few who got kicked out for using. The men sometimes harassed the girls.

Sister Betty wasn't sure that she felt up to hosting this month. She had been sleeping fitfully recently and had been experiencing headaches. She was looking forward to the month being over. She had even petitioned her superiors to take the first week of January off. The church had a cabin on Bainbridge Island, and she was looking forward to the retreat.

The night before the guests were to arrive, Sister Betty walked down the staircase to find a young woman sitting in the reception area. She sat alone on the yellow vinyl couch, the statue of the Blessed Mother looking beatifically down on her. As Sister Betty reached the base of the staircase, she saw that her assistant had left for the evening.

"May I help you?" Sister Betty asked.

The girl looked up. She had a broad, open face. Her hair was dirty brown, cut into a messy shag. She had silver half-moon earrings and a purple peasant top on. "Are you Betty Holland?" the young woman asked.

This was unusual. It was infrequent that she was asked for by her secular name. "I'm Sister Betty Holland," she replied, feeling at once formal and self-conscious.

The girl's face lit up. "I've been looking for you. Did you use to live at Shadow Rock?"

"And you are?" Sister Betty asked. "I didn't get your name?"

"Oh, sorry." The girl stood up and extended her hand. "My name is Ruby West. I'm a student at Pacific Community College. I want to go to film school eventually, if I can pull the money together. Anyway, I'm trying to put together a documentary about the place I grew up. And I found some research that had your name in it. Didn't you live there once?"

"You're putting together a documentary about this place?" Sister Betty asked.

"Yes, I hope to. I went back earlier this year. I hadn't been there since I was ten. Anyway, I filmed some footage and interviewed people there. But I'm trying to find some outsiders who could offer their perspective. From the research I've done, it seems that you lived there for a while."

Sister Betty felt cornered. Despite her youthful demeanor, her visitor seemed to mean business. "You must be looking for a different Betty Holland," she said. "It's a fairly common name. I'm sorry you've come all this way for nothing. Now if you'll excuse me, this is a busy time."

Sister Betty turned and walked quickly away. As she shut the door to her office, she saw a figure through the glass: Ruby had gotten up and followed her. Now she stood in front of the office door, rapping her hand on the frosted window. Her arm was distorted through the amber glass, looking like a tree branch.

When Sister Betty did nothing, she knocked again, insistently.

After a few moments, standing in the dark of her office, Sister Betty saw the figure move away from the door. She waited until she heard the front door slam shut before she moved from her spot in the middle of the room.

● ● ●

Ren walked across the padded floors at the Lone Wolf Self Defense Center, stretching as she went. She hadn't been to class since the Capitol Hill case opened, but recently had more time on her hands. She had been spending her evenings reading detective novels to get her mind off her life. Her favorites were a series about a fortune-teller in New Orleans who also solved crimes. Amateur sleuths had it best. They could violate every rule.

The case still wasn't closed officially, but it was looking like it would be soon. Lieutenant Roemer was leaning toward the murder/suicide theory, and she wanted to have the matter settled by the New Year. Ren and Sean were spending their workdays trying to identify the young man that died near the Vashon ferries, and also trying to find more information on

Cedar from her classmates at Seattle South high school, where she had been a student until the previous winter. She had taken a leave when her mother got sick and never returned. She died a dropout.

Ren took a place at the back of the room. Sifu Pearl was absent tonight, and in her place a burly Japanese woman with a thick neck and a buzz cut was instructing them. Class was just about to begin when Ren heard someone say her name.

Barreling across the mats was Stella Hadley. Ren hadn't seen her since the first night of the crime. Stella waved a hello, and shot her a glance midway through the class. When Thick-Necked Substitute rang the small gong at the end of the hour, Stella made a beeline over.

Ren had no desire to chitchat. During their Academy days, Stella and Ren had been close, united by their outcast status in the macho environment. They went out for lunch and drinks often back then. Stella had always shown pointed interest in Ren's life, asking probing questions and following up on them without prompting.

Ren had confessed more than she should have and soon regretted her lack of discretion. Stella was the kind of person who was always poking around in other people's lives, trying to convince herself that they were downtrodden. It made her feel better about herself. She was a perfect fit for social work, where she spent her days around the less fortunate. It was all a huge ego boost for her.

"I didn't expect to see you in Skyway," Stella said. Her voice always sounded like she had a cold. "I bought a house last year over on Sandpiper. I gotta tell you, I don't love the neighborhood. The family to one side has a dismantled car on their front lawn and see nothing wrong with it. And the couple on the other side keeps inviting me to their church. I think the people out this way are what my mother would call *common*."

"I'm in a bit of a rush," Ren said and walked quickly toward the changing room. Stella followed her into it. "I have to get back to the city."

"I need to tell you, Ren, I heard this crazy rumor."

Ren stripped out of her kung fu clothes. She didn't mind being half-naked around Stella; she had seen it all in their Academy days. She rolled on some deodorant, changed her bra, and started to pack her bag: keys, cell, slip-on shoes. She was planning to stop by Sanctuary for a drink. She had burned enough for one cocktail. "Stella, I have to tell you, I'm not really into gossip. I find it kind of tedious."

"I think you're going to want to hear this," Stella said.

Ren pulled on a pair of baggy jeans and a black top. She ran a comb through her long, black hair. It was the one thing she had gotten from her father: his Cherokee mane. Students at Veronica Prep used to call her Pocahontas.

Ren felt the need to take the path of least resistance. It was her only way out of this. "What it is you heard?"

Stella exhaled, emitting nicotine and stale peppermint. "My coworker called me into her office the other day. She's been looking to hire an investigator to look into fraud issues that come up. You know, people filing false welfare claims and such. Anyway, she placed an ad and interviewed a few people for the job. She was looking for my recommendation. Guess who her lead candidate is?"

Ren shook her head. She had no idea where Stella was going with this.

"Sean Lukela," Stella said with a flourish. She arched her eyebrow.

Ren's heart accelerated. She felt slightly dizzy. "You're telling me this, why?"

"Did you know that your partner is looking to leave the precinct?"

Ren slammed her locker shut and threw her bag over her shoulder. She would call the school tomorrow to ask which classes Stella Hadley was registered for. It was her plan to avoid her from now on. "Yes, of course I knew. Sean keeps me informed."

She left the room without another word.

Driving back into the city, Ren blared the radio. Some woman with a lion's mane of auburn hair and big, red lips was singing about being the last on someone's list. Over the music, Ren's thoughts settled on one question: *Sean, why are you leaving me?*

CHAPTER TWELVE

Lydia Merton stepped into her living room and had to resist the impulse to spin around from the sheer joy of it. It was the first week of December, and she had finally been given clearance by Seattle Police to move back into her house. "I wish I could carry myself across the threshold," she told the officer who let her back in. He nodded and left her alone.

She was flush with energy, running up and down the stairs. The house had been thoroughly cleansed by an environmental cleanup crew. There were seals across her toilets and sinks. It all had a fresh, slightly antiseptic feeling to it. Still, Lydia was thrilled to be home. She had missed the house the way you miss a person. She couldn't wait to build a fire, to bathe in her own tub, to bake some sinful Christmas treats.

Lydia hadn't seen David since they got back from Alberta. The best she had managed, in the days since her first interrogation, was a brief call via the main line at the Westside Home on one of his days on staff. They both suspected that detectives were shadowing them and that their phones were being monitored, even before the police had confirmed it. The case had made their relationship even more furtive, and she feared lasting damage.

Lydia pushed the dark thoughts out of her mind. Moving home was the first good thing that had happened to her since she got back from Lake Louise, and she was determined to make the most of it.

First up, she would do her laundry. She dumped the contents of her suitcase and the Hefty bag on her living room rug.

She almost wanted to burn her clothes, but she was simply was too prudent for an impulse like that.

Lydia opened her stereo and put on a CD. Soon Pearl Jam was blaring from the speakers, singing about Jeremy and inconsolable losses. Once Lydia had yearned for Eddie Vedder the way she currently did for David Skarda. Not surprising, she thought. They were both mysterious and un-attainable.

Lydia started with a small wash, piling things up in a plastic hamper. She trundled the basket downstairs. There was a washer and dryer in the basement, along with a workbench overcrowded with every gadget under the sun. She let Hector deal with them. The only items she recognized were some crusty paintbrushes and a spotted smock from a project she'd done the previous summer.

Her basement was always a mess, and that remained un-changed. There were stacks of empty boxes that she planned to reuse, empty jars for future canning projects, heaps of Sty-rofoam peanuts for packing. Most of this was piled up haphaz-ardly on an old chrome bar set, which had once been found in the rec room. Years ago, people had entertained here. It was hard to imagine. Ever since Lydia moved in, it had looked like the county dump.

The forensic team had removed her basement door for testing. They had replaced it with a remarkably similar rep-lica, especially given that the original door was many years old. She was impressed. Lydia had never heard back from detec-tives about the fingerprint they had isolated on the door. She assumed that they knew now it was David's.

Lydia sorted the first load into the washer. She measured some soap. As she poured, blue detergent spilled into the hamper.

"Fuck!" she blurted, glad that David couldn't hear her. He

didn't like cursing. She tried to wipe up the mess at the bottom of the basket, but it was useless. After a moment, she had a thought. There was an identical clothes hamper behind the chrome bar. It was placed on the floor to align with her laundry chute, found behind a door upstairs.

She walked over, moving aside a large tarp that was on the ground. She stepped back behind the bar. Some empty cartons and bags of peanuts had fallen onto the area. She moved them aside.

Here it was: her chute hamper. She leaned down to grab some clothing that had been left in it. It was her winter coat, the one she had forgotten to take on the Lake Louise trip. It had a tapestry design with black and white swirls. She had worn it for years. But what was it doing here?

Lydia lifted it up. It had a noticeable stain on the right side. A garlicky smell wafted over to her. She moved over into available light. It dawned on her that the girl must have worn her coat when she was staying in the house. She must have dropped it down the chute after she soiled it. The police missed it, which wasn't hard to imagine. The laundry chute was hidden upstairs behind a door. It would be easy to miss if you didn't know it was there.

Lydia dug her hand into one of the coat pockets. She pulled out some loose change: silver mostly, less than a dollar. There was also a small copper object, an almond shape. She held it up. It showed an image of a dragon, with "Chinatown 2011" stamped on it.

Lydia rummaged in the other pocket. There was some kind of paper in it, folded several times. When she pulled it out, she realized it was an envelope that had been creased into squares. She uncurled it. There was a stamp and a postmark: from Seattle earlier that year. The envelope was addressed to a woman named Cedar Heekin at an address near the airport.

It was what Lydia saw in the upper-left corner that gave her pause. She looked at it again, scarcely believing her eyes.

The return address was in a familiar handwriting. It read 731 21st Ave. East, Seattle, WA 98112. There was a name scrawled above the return, one she recognized.

Lydia had sent the letter.

CHAPTER THIRTEEN

Ren stood in front of the house on Aloha, hardly believing that she was here again. The structure hadn't changed demonstrably in fifteen years. It was a black half-timber that reminded Ren of a ski lodge. On the front lawn, three pine trees stood together as if in consultation. The grass had dried into islands of sallow. It was the one thing that kept Ren from slipping back in time to her eighteen-year-old self: since she had last been there, the Mafia Manor had gone to seed.

That is what they had called it, back in the day. Del claimed that her father ran her life as if he were the head of one of the Five Families. At the height of her drug binges, he tapped her phone, had her dealers put in jail, and kidnapped her in the middle of the night, all in an effort to get her off the rock. None of it helped. Del had been in and out of addiction since the age of sixteen, and on and off the streets since graduation.

When Hattie Mott called the previous day to tell Ren that Del's recent activity was at the house on Aloha, she had been dubious. If there were one constant in Del's life, other than her addiction, it was her estrangement from her father. She hated her stepmother. But it made sense now: Milton and Christiana weren't at the house much anymore. They seemed to have abandoned it.

Ren rang the doorbell and waited. She had visions of the interior: cavernous empty rooms, with tables bare, save for glass pipes and drug paraphernalia. Perhaps Del had gotten into dealing. Maybe it wasn't she who had broken onto the houseboat but one of her derelict friends. Ren had a small handgun on her just in case.

When the door opened, Ren nearly gasped. Del stood there, smirking. It took Ren only one look to realize that Del was clean.

"You got my signal, I take it," Del said.

"It was hard to miss."

They stood for a moment in silence, sizing each other up like Puck and Ariel on a bad day.

"You rang?" It was a statement more than a question.

"You told me your door would always be open to me," Del responded. "That's why you gave me the key."

It was true. Ren had said that to her four years ago, when Del was being shipped off to rehab in Arizona. It was the fifth program Milton had sent her to. Ren hadn't heard from her since.

Del looked amazing. Since the last time Ren had seen her, she had gained weight and had her teeth fixed. She was dressed all in white right now, just like the days at Veronica Prep. It was a color that did wonders for her tan skin and dark hair.

"I was coming to tell you something," Del said.

"What's that?" Ren asked.

"I wanted to say good-bye."

•   •   •

Father David Skarda sat on a park bench. In the distance teenagers played tennis, knocking balls back and forth over a loose net. Women walked by with babies in strollers. The sun was out, and so were the residents of Capitol Hill. It wasn't the best time to be meeting in public, but Lydia had made it sound urgent. In his hand, Father Skarda held a letter. He looked at it, reading it again:

April 8, 2011

Dear Ms. Heekin:

Thank you for your letter. It's not often that I hear from prospective students. I commend you for looking ahead to your college years and planning your academics in advance. I think Pacific Community College will be lucky to have you.

In answer to your query, I did teach a class at Pacific called Alternative Religious Communities in the US. Unfortunately, the class was not popular, and I only had the chance to teach it once, several years ago now. There are no plans to resurrect the course as far as I know. I'm surprised it's still listed on the PCC website. You'd be amazed at all the problems we have with technology here!

I'm not sure what you mean by your question, "How did you learn about these communities?" I do have a degree in comparative and alternative religion from the Evergreen State College. I would imagine that is where I first learned of these places. Hope that answers your question.

Since you expressed such a keen interest, I have enclosed an old copy of the syllabus. It will give you the reading list and a sense of what the class was about.

Good luck with your final year of high school.

Sincerely,

Lydia Merton

After he read it a second time, he said, "This is why they say no good deed goes unpunished."

Lydia smiled. He could always make her feel better.

"I can see why you're spooked, Lyd. But you have to see the blessing here too. This does settle a nagging question. Now you know how she knew where you lived."

"But that's nothing. It does nothing to explain why did this girl broke into my house."

"I don't know, darling. I've worked with enough street kids to know that they do all kinds of desperate things. Some sell their bodies; others befriend people just to scam them out of pocket change. There are some really sad kids in this city. I wouldn't overthink this."

"But I sent that letter to an address. I don't think she was homeless."

"Maybe not last April. But to squat in someone's house? You've got to be desperate."

A gust of wind blew, scattering some raindrops from the trees overhead. Lydia moved a bit closer to David. "I'm trying to decide what to do. I don't feel like doing the police any favors."

"You have to turn this in, Lydia. It's evidence. The coat you found it in too. There might be DNA on it."

"But it makes me look guilty. I had forgotten all about writing that letter. I never once made the connection. What if they think I've been deliberately withholding information?"

"You answered someone's letter nine months ago. They'll believe that you forgot about it. They'll be so happy to have this stuff that they'll be on your side for once."

"Are they going to believe I found this stuff in my house? That makes them look incompetent."

"Don't think of it that way. Think it as something that might settle this case, once and for all. To hold this back would be unethical."

She mused for a moment. "You're right," she said finally. "OK, I will turn it in."

There was a pause. Then David said, "I'm glad you called me. I was going a bit crazy not seeing you."

She looked at him with tenderness. "I think we need to do our Christmas celebration again this year, to hell with the sneaking around. The detectives know about us; it's pointless to act like they don't."

David looked back at her, a twinkle in his eye. "I see a pot roast dinner in our future, darling. Just the two of us."

In the distance, a foghorn sounded.

"How is Jakob?" David asked her.

Lydia bristled. She hated it when David brought him up. "I don't know. He seems to have dropped my class. I haven't seen him in a while."

"Lovers' quarrel?"

"More than that. I think it's over."

"Another coed who couldn't stand the test of time."

"Something like that."

"How are you feeling about it being over?"

Lydia looked at him sharply. She deliberated for a moment before she continued. "David, I know it was your idea that I see other men. But do you think it's maybe a little odd that we talk about it?"

David rested his hand on her leg. It was the most affection he'd shown her today. "I want you to be happy, darling. You can't subsist on a few weekends a year with me; you know that."

It was a well-worn topic. David was married to Rome. The most he could offer her was their annual weekend away and a few days here and there throughout the year. He wanted Lydia to enjoy herself when he wasn't around.

The first few years they were together Lydia had been incensed every time he brought it up. It was insulting. She didn't care about his commitment to Rome; she was devoted only to him. But over time she had begun to see his point. They would never have a life in the traditional sense. Lydia began to go on a few dates here and there. David had pushed Jakob on her the previous winter; the kid was from one of the church's group homes. He was an orphan who showed academic promise. David got him a spot at PCC and a date with Lydia.

None of it really worked, though. Spending time with other men merely reinforced how rare and special her love was for David. Perhaps he knew this on some level. It may have been his own calculated way of staying first in her heart.

"I have to go," David said. "Mrs. Longo is making me meatballs for lunch. We're going to watch *Vertigo*." He picked up a briefcase, which was resting at his feet. It was a communion kit for the old women he visited on days like today.

Lydia felt a twinge of jealousy. The old Italian women of Capitol Hill saw more of David than she did. She wanted to object, tell him to blow off his obligations and spend the day at home with her. She opened her mouth to protest, but found that she didn't have words for it. She was conditioned by their years together: think it, don't say it.

Without another word between them, he was gone.

CHAPTER FOURTEEN

"To bright futures," Fiona cheered, holding her martini glass aloft. It was late afternoon, and she was toasting her second pomegranate cosmo. Around the table were the remains of fried calamari and seared blue fish. They were at Seahorse, a few blocks from the office. The light was fading as they finished up the farewell lunch. Ruby's internship was winding up as the Christmas holidays approached. It seemed as good a time as any for her to depart, since their investigation had stalled.

They had been working tirelessly for two months, trying to break open the Capitol Hill case. Fiona's goal was to solve the case before the police did. She had spent many afternoons picking up the check after lunches with potential leads, but all she had gotten was a swelling credit card balance. If the Seattle Police had procured any witnesses, those individuals appeared to be heeding the admonishment not to talk to the press about it.

All of this was frustrating and precarious. This case only had the potential to be marketable if the murderer turned out to be as interesting as the strange details of the murder. If they did all this work only to discover that some junkie stabbed the girl for pocket change, Fiona had just spent thousands of dollars on a story that few people would care about. She had her reputation, as well as her finances, to consider. Fiona Swift was on a mission.

Ruby West had proven to be her best resource. She ordinarily had reservations about hiring interns, but Ruby had stood out from the crowd. Once she had signed on, she was invaluable. She had gone undercover at her school, posing as a former student of Lydia Merton's to try to learn more about her. She had provided Fiona with a trove of background information on her, including her impression of what type of person she thought Lydia was.

Unfortunately, Lydia Merton appeared to be a singularly boring person. She wouldn't make a particularly compelling subject, according to Ruby. From what Fiona could make out herself, this was true. Lydia had a college degree, taught religion, and seemed to be a bit of a spinster. She wouldn't sell copy.

They walked back from Seahorse to the office, a bracing six blocks in a bitter north wind. "I could use some help before you leave today," Fiona said. "I need to update my site immediately."

Ruby nodded. Fiona had no technical skills whatsoever. Ruby had been doing a lot of the website content since her internship began.

Fiona stepped into the shade of a building and lit a cigarette with her Zippo lighter. She inhaled deeply. "And don't forget I have your letter of recommendation. Tish should have it ready for you by the time you leave."

They got back to the office, a fifth-floor walkup with views of Pike Place Market. Fiona's assistant, Tish, was playing Angry Birds as they entered. She shut off her handheld and dropped it into the top drawer.

"Tish, can you go get me a coffee?" Fiona said, hanging up her overcoat. Fiona was dressed in London Fog and Coach leather. She could have been a print ad. "A strong blend, low caffeine."

Ruby took a seat at Fiona's desk. In the distance she saw the red, illuminated sign for Pike Place Market. She went there occasionally to browse around. Fishmongers tossed their catch back and forth and shouted limericks. Hippies sold bracelets and incense. You could visit the first Starbucks and drink your coffee with a view of the Space Needle. It was an invented reality of Seattle life.

Ruby fiddled away for a few minutes with the Word file, setting up text and doing a preliminary upload. She called Fiona over to approve it.

"You are a genius," Fiona said.

Ruby stood up quickly and moved away. "Fiona, have you given any more thought to what I asked you?"

Fiona looked at her blankly. What had they discussed?

"Remember I asked you if I could run a banner ad on your webpage, promoting my site?"

"Oh, yes. You wanted to do this, why?"

"Because it's great publicity for my site, for one thing. I can set it up in a few minutes if you give me the go-ahead. I would really appreciate it."

Fiona squinted at her. This girl had a drive and ambition she had noticed right away when she met her the previous summer. She reminded Fiona a bit of herself. "What is your site about?" she asked her.

"It's meant to promote a documentary I'm making. It's about a commune I lived in until I was ten. I went back there to solve a mystery from my early childhood."

"Oh right, you want to go to film school, and this documentary is your ticket in." It was all coming back to her now.

"Let me show you," the girl said. She pulled a laptop out of her shoulder bag and powered up. It was a relic over ten years old that had once belonged to her father. The first thing she planned to do with her bounty was to buy a replacement. She had a backache from lugging this one around.

Ruby opened an application. Fiona walked over and peered down at the screen. Entering the site, there was a sea-foam green background. Some tinny, creepy music played as an intro. After a moment, words shot out at the viewer. One by one, in black script:

WHAT

HAPPENED

AT

SHADOW

ROCK

A large question mark shot out last, shattering all the words like glass. All it was missing was that sound effect. The screen went back to solid sea-foam green. A few headings had been set up. Fiona clicked on a few. They were empty.

"I'm still working on the content of the site," the girl said. "But it won't hurt to test the waters, see if the ad alone generates interest and speculation."

Fiona looked at her intern, invested. "What did happen at Shadow Rock, Ruby?"

She smiled at her. "Let me put up the ad, and I'll tell you."

Ruby had moxie. It was rare in a girl her age. Fiona waved her arm in approval. "Go to it."

Ruby got to work, setting up the ad. It took her a while, longer than she had claimed it would. Fiona left the office for a while, drank her coffee while talking to Tish at her desk, and then came back. She took a seat in the visitor's chair and checked her Blackberry.

Finally, Ruby was finished. The banner ad was live. Ruby jumped up from the desk, clapping gleefully as she looked at the update.

"So," Fiona said, taking back her spot. Ruby had left the seat warm. "What did happen at Shadow Rock, anyway?"

Ruby looked at her, teasingly. "Promise not to tell?" she said.

• • •

There were a few things that Ren had come to expect of Delphine Hutching. One was that Del did nothing that didn't ultimately serve her own purposes. Ren had learned this about her long ago. Clean or using, Del was a bit of a weasel.

So when Del told her that she had visited the houseboat to say good-bye, Ren knew it was a half-lie. There was something else Del was after. She was a bad detective for not spotting right away what it was.

None of this awareness kept Ren from falling back in bed with her. This was another thing she knew to be true: whenever Del resurfaced, they hit the sheets. Ren refused to feel shame about this. Contrary to all the popular bullshit out there, sex is a hard thing to come by. Ren had only ever found three women she felt compelled to get bare with. Sex was one of those rare events in her life, like a visit to Temple or her weight dipping below one forty-five.

When she awoke in a large sleigh bed in the house on Aloha, she was naked under the duvet. The memory of Del was all over her: on her lips, her breasts, and at points beyond. She hadn't been in this room before. There was a large art nouveau fireplace facing the bed and a brass chandelier over it. The room was empty of anything else.

"I can't believe you met my buddy Owl," Del said, coming into the room. She was dressed in white again, but had pulled on a brown cable knit sweater. She took a seat on the duvet, crossing her feet Indian style. "Get this, he used to be a professor at some school in the Midwest. He has a PhD in medieval literature."

Ren wasn't surprised somehow. She had seen what addiction did to people. Looking around the room now, she couldn't believe that Del had given all this up to live on the streets. Del had told her once that living loaded on the streets was easier than living clean under Milton's thumb.

Del reached over and kissed Ren. Her lips were thick like caterpillars. "Promise me something," she said. She took Ren's hand in hers and linked their fingers together.

"What?"

"That woman you mentioned yesterday, that crush of yours. I want you to ask her out."

Ren shook her head. "It's impractical. She's a single mother, for one thing. I don't even know if she's gay. I just suspect it."

"Just try it, Ren. The worst that can happen is that you'll end up back where you are now. That's what I used to tell myself when I was sleeping under the Bainbridge overpass."

Ren nodded, burying her head in Del's soft hair. No matter how much she fought this, she loved this woman. She wondered if other people felt this peculiar mix of tender love and bitter disappointment when spending time with the one they loved. She hoped not.

Del stood up. She walked tentatively, as if she needed a cane. "Come with me. I want to show you something."

They moved through the house. It was cavernous and cold, as if it were calling out for the heat of objects. Del led Ren by the hand down a set of heavy oak stairs into the basement. The area was filled with easels and oils, boxes of colored sea glass and buttons. There was one chair, covered with a white spackled tarp. This seemed to be where Del was spending her time since coming home.

"I've been working with paper," Del said, moving over the cement floor. To one side, there were scraps of newspaper all over the ground. Some were painted white, black, and red.

"You'll need this," Del said, disappearing for a few moments before emerging with a small stepladder. She placed it at the foot of the paper collage and then held Ren's hand as she took a few steps up.

"Do you see it?" Del asked.

Ren scrutinized the floor. It was a mass of newspaper scraps—some painted, some not. It was like looking at an incomplete jigsaw puzzle.

"Take another few steps, up to the top. I'll hold onto you."

Ren did as she was told, wobbling at bit as she reached the top. She looked down at the floor. The scraps of paper now formed a face. "Wow," she said. "That's amazing."

"What do you see?" Del asked.

"It looks like the cover of *Tattoo You*," Ren said. "My mother would plotz if she knew I remembered what it looked like." She considered it again. "Or maybe an androgynous female face. An androgynous female model."

"I like your theories," Del said. "You can step down."

After they went back upstairs. Del built a fire and they settled into a red velvet couch in front of it. She pulled out a carved ivory pipe and filled it. "Don't worry, it's just tobacco," she said. "You'd be amazed how much I miss the inhale. This helps a bit."

"So where are your parents, anyway?"

Del exhaled smoke, coughing as she did. "Last I heard, Christiana was in Argentina and Milton was fucking some woman in Telluride. But they're going to be back before I know it. I can smell my father in the air."

"I was so surprised when I heard you were staying here. You're getting along with Milton again?" Once upon a time, Del had been daddy's little girl. Ren had heard the stories, but have never seen any sign of it.

Del grinned. "He thinks we are. That's the beauty of it."

"So that's why you're leaving," Ren said. Nothing much had changed. It made more sense now.

"It's my only shot. Get gone before they come back. They won't know where to find me this time."

"You really believe that?" Ren asked. "You said it yourself: Milton is like the godfather. Alaska is full of people looking to profit from turning someone in."

Del lit the pipe one last time. "That's where you come in, my friend."

Here it was, the primary reason Del had come courting. The secondary one Ren was starting to regret.

"I'm not doing anything to jeopardize my job. You know that," Ren said.

"You won't need to."

"What is it, then?"

Del smiled contentedly. Or was it a smirk? "I need you to find out everything you can about a woman named Jude Hamlin," she said.

CHAPTER FIFTEEN

Father Skarda lifted the piece of meat, looking like a mother raising a newborn. It was six pounds of pork, decadent for a pre-holiday meal, but he felt they deserved it. He lay the cut down in a shallow roasting pan. It could wait.

Lydia was across the room, chopping onions and carrots. She took a sip of wine, warmed. This was a holiday of sorts for them, their tenth together. They never could celebrate on December 25, given the nature of his work, but they found a way to honor the season in their own way. Tonight it was pork roast, Swedish potatoes, and a Queen of Sheba cake for dessert.

Lydia opened a few drawers, puzzled. "I don't think the crime lab replaced my knives," she said. "This one I'm using is dull."

"Looks OK to me," David said, surveying her heap of vegetables.

They moved to the front room, carrying the cabernet bottle with them. Lydia had drawn the blinds. Ordinarily they didn't socialize in the front room, but since the incident the TV room, with its plush red sofa, seemed tainted.

Lydia had built a fire, and it was sparking. *Abbey Road* was on the stereo. David was a fan, not Lydia. He had wide musical taste, everyone from the Stones to Jerry Garcia. It had been years since she listened to music regularly, but in high school she was a grunge fan.

After they sat for a while, David pulled out an envelope and handed it to Lydia.

"Are we exchanging gifts now?" Lydia asked. "I've still got some wrapping to do."

"Go ahead," he said. "I can wait."

She ripped open her gift. Inside was a travel brochure.

"Jackson," she said. The image of the snow-capped Tetons, reflected in a pool of still water, was lovely.

"What do you think?" he asked her.

"Sounds perfect to me."

This was their ritual. Every Christmas he picked out the location for their next trip. It gave them something to look forward to all year. Given how infrequently they saw each other, they needed it. He had done well so far with his selection of getaway spots: Zion the first year, Joshua Tree the next, then Savannah, Ojai, Vancouver, New Orleans, and Lake Louise. They had missed the two years Lydia was in grad school in the Bay Area, content to meet up in the city there.

"Splendid," she said. They sat side-by-side watching the fire. He had his hand on her knee.

"Have the police been in touch with you at all recently?" he asked her after a time.

"Not recently," she said. "It's starting to feel like this is going away."

"I think so too," he said. "The new year can be a fresh start in more ways than one."

She smiled, feeling content, and said nothing.

"What did the police say when you turned in that letter you found?" he asked her. He dipped to the floor and picked up the cabernet bottle, emptying the contents into her glass.

"They thanked me," she lied. "But not much else."

"And the coat?" he asked.

"They took it to the lab. I don't know anything more than that. They're not exactly in the business of giving out information."

He nodded. "I'll give the Seattle Police credit; this case has been airtight so far. No leaks to the press about her identity, or about mine."

"I know," Lydia said. "We've been lucky."

After a few moments, David got up and resumed his work in the kitchen. Lydia stayed put, listening to him clatter around.

The letter to Cedar Heekin and the coat were still with her stuff, upstairs. She trusted David not to snoop. She couldn't quite face the police yet, although she would eventually.

In the meantime, Lydia had more pressing issues to worry about. The girl had been calling her, a lot. She wanted to talk to her about something. She was half expecting her to do another drop-in, during office hours.

Lydia sat back, finishing her last bit of red wine. She was thinking things through. She hadn't decided yet what to do about Ruby West.

CHAPTER SIXTEEN

Sean Lukela closed the sliding glass door with a firm thud. His rottweiler, Maggie, paced the deck outside, sniffing the breeze. The three large buckets of pork BBQ on the kitchen counter were driving her wild. Sean had picked up the food from Khan's on his way back from work, along with some large sweet rolls from the bakery. The guys could make themselves sandwiches when they arrived. He was expecting Sid and Jason, and Jasper from the crime lab. Henry Wu had called to say he was running late.

Sean lived in a single-story ranch house in Skyway. It looked not unlike the house he had grown up in. His family had moved to Seattle when he was in third grade and his sister in kindergarten. Their father had gotten a job as an inspector at Boeing, so they had moved to the mainland. It took Sean most of that year to convince his classmates that he wasn't some shirtless island boy who had moved from a land where he lived in a grass hut and fished for his dinner. To mainlanders, native Hawaiians were as peculiar as exotic birds.

Since that time, Sean had started to think of the Pacific Northwest as home. He would always be an outsider, but he loved his adopted city. He had a house, a job, and occasionally some lady luck. It could be a lot worse.

As he waited for the guys to arrive, Sean noticed the light blinking on his home answering machine. He got to it a lot less often than his cell phone. He hit the play button. Some telemarketer robots were first, then a neighbor complaining that Maggie had dug into her lettuce patches. The third was curious: cackling and whizzing and a child's voice. He waited for the fourth.

"Hey, bro. Sorry about that last message. Keala hit speed dial when I was out of the room. I was just checking in to see if you're going to visit Mom and Dad over the holidays. I was looking at flights to Honolulu, and they're about seven hundred. Let me know what your plans are."

Sean erased the message. He would talk to his sister later. She lived just a few blocks over with his three-year-old niece. Sean's family was not religious, and if they had been they would have been Buddhist on his mother's side. But ever since Keala had come along, the family did a secular Christmas with presents and stockings. Sean had told Keala that Santa would show up on a surfboard this year.

He wasn't sure he could take the time off this year, though. Money was tight, and the case was ongoing. The thought of spending the holidays alone in rainy Seattle was depressing as hell to him.

The doorbell rang, and Maggie went nuts in the backyard. Sean ignored her and walked through the living room, past the fake fireplace and the poker table he had set up for tonight.

"Dude, I don't think your neighbor lady likes brothers," Sid said as he made his way in. He had a six-pack of Blue Moon under his arm. "She was staring at me like I was one of America's Most Wanted. I wish I had my badge with me; I could have had some fun with her."

"She doesn't like anyone," Sean said, taking the beer from him. "I think she would poison Maggie if she could get away with it."

Sid made his way into the kitchen and had a look around. "It smells awesome in here. I can't wait to beat your ass tonight."

Sean pulled some plates and napkins from the cupboard.

"Any chance your hottie sister will be stopping by tonight?" Sid asked. He arched an eyebrow and guffawed.

Sean shook his head and said nothing. Guys were always after his sister, even repressed homosexuals like Sid Hopkins.

The doorbell rang again, and Jason and Jasper entered. They had arrived at the same time. Jason brought Fat Tire and Jasper three pints of Ben and Jerry's.

They went about assembling their sandwiches. Henry Wu showed up twenty minutes later with a bottle of Jägermeister.

"Dude, have you wagered on the baby yet?" Sid asked Sean, taking a swig from a bottle. "We've got five hundred in the pot. Nola says she'll give it up for my Hanukkah gift."

Sid claimed to be Jewish on his mother's side, a detail no one questioned. He also claimed that he could ask three simple questions and determine a person's sexual history. So far he had proven his track record on that one. He had been the first one, years ago, to point out to the guys that Ren and Stella Hadley were both gay.

Sean had mixed feelings about the wager. Placing a bet on the father of someone's kid was tawdry, especially when it was the boss. He went to his bedroom and examined his wallet. He pulled out five twenties and returned. He walked back into the kitchen, handed the bills over to Sid, and told him his guess.

It would be the easiest five hundred Sean had ever made. He felt mildly guilty for not giving it up, but a bet was a bet. He could use his winnings to see his family over the holidays. The truth was, Sean didn't need to guess. The money was already his. He knew who the father of Lieutenant Roemer's baby was.

CHAPTER SEVENTEEN

Ren careened through Crown Hill in her Camaro, hitting inclines the vehicle could barely handle. It was the first night of Hanukkah, and Ren was getting to her destination in the nick of time. She had picked up Ramon, who had closed Sanctuary for the night. This event was a long-standing Copeland family tradition: dinner at Bebe's apartment at sundown. Every year they shared prayers, songs, the lighting of the first candle, and an exchange of gifts.

Bebe lived in a mustard-colored building with a bell tower that had once belonged to the Catholic Church. Her rent-controlled apartment took up most of the top floor. Ren and Ramon could still enter their childhood bedrooms, frozen in time like an exhibit at the Smithsonian. No matter how many men had come in and out of Bebe's life, the family home had stayed the same. That was critical to her.

There was an ornate gilded elevator in the lobby. Today there was a sign on it that said, "No Work." Ren and her brother headed for the wide-set staircase instead. The interior hadn't changed in thirty years. There were the embossed crosses on the newel posts and the high ceilings that created a feeling of cloistered quiet. This building could be downright creepy at times.

"Don't forget. You owe me sixty dollars," Ramon said, as they reached the top floor. He had found the perfect gift for their mother: a Ramones poster from a show at the Fillmore in 1978. Their parents had attended the show on their honeymoon. Once upon a time, they had been big enough fans to name their son after the band. Ramon had paid to have the poster framed. It was currently wrapped in silver and blue paper in a shopping bag.

Bebe answered the door, resplendent in lapis. The apartment sparkled, as it always did on these occasions. There was a fire in the fireplace, chamber music on the turntable. The signs of Bebe's normal life—easels and stacks of vinyl—had been cleared away. The kitchen table had been moved to the center of the living room, draped in blue cloth. A menorah stood at the center. Bebe had fixed gift bags for her kids with seven presents to take with them when they left. An eighth, which they would open tonight, sat on their chairs.

"Did Ramon tell you we saw Harlot's Web a few nights ago?" Bebe asked as she made her way back to the kitchen. She had been washing some green beans when the doorbell rang. "You should have come."

"It was an amazing show," Ramon said, trailing behind them. He removed a corkscrew from a drawer and opened a bottle of pinot noir. "They have this song called 'Rachel Jaded' that is just...." He was apparently at a loss for words, because he said nothing.

"God," Bebe said, reliving the moment. "They just nailed it."

"The band stops by the bar occasionally. You really should meet them. The lead singer is hot. And the drummer...."

"I was going to wait to tell you over dessert," Ren said. "I've been seeing Delphine again. She's clean and off the streets. She's really turned her life around. So I am not really looking for any setups."

They both looked at her, surprised and curious.

"You have the chance to date RJ Simon, and the person you really want is Del again?" Ramon said. Her mother and brother just didn't get the Del fascination. Never had, never would.

"I knew you weren't going to be thrilled, but I thought you deserved to know. And don't fret. She's leaving soon. Moving to Anchorage. We aren't dating; we're just hanging out."

Mother and son exchanged a glance. Ramon left the kitchen and was soon tooling around with the turntable. Bebe returned to stringing the beans.

Ren's growing-up years had been about this apartment: her mother and her brother, and her memories of Bebe's parents. These were the forces that had shaped her. Standing here on the warped wooden floors of the kitchen, she could remember eating Cheerios out of a blue ceramic bowl on a chilly school day, rushing with wet hair to catch the bus to Queen Anne. She could step into her bedroom and see her photos and trophies from her high school days, or leaf through her yellow-spined Nancy Drews.

"I miss my parents on nights like this," Bebe said. She had pulled the brisket out of the oven and was basting it. The smell of oil and mixed herbs filled the air. "They could always pull it together for the holidays. Put their differences aside so that we enjoyed ourselves. That can't have been easy to do, given what went on between them."

Ren's granddad was thick in the middle and wore big glasses. When she visited his nightclub as a girl, he brought her 7UP and cherry juice in a lowball.

"When did they get divorced, anyway? I don't even remember them together."

"Just a few years before bubbe died. She finally had enough and wanted to spend her last years alone. That took guts for someone from her generation."

"Heart of Gold" began thumping from the living room speakers. Ramon joined them.

"You couldn't have selected more appropriate music, son?"

He shrugged.

"I think we're ready to eat," Bebe said. "Is the bread on the table?"

Ramon nodded dutifully. Bebe lifted the brisket from the roasting pan and placed it on a silver platter.

Ren's phone rang. She excused herself to the hallway when she saw who was calling.

"Sean, did you forget that tonight is a holiday for me?" she asked. She was slightly irked at her partner. He could be thoughtless at times.

"No, Ren, I didn't. I'm sorry to be interrupting. It's an emergency."

"What is it?" she asked, although she could already sense his words before she heard them.

"There has been another murder," he told her.

• • •

When Ren got to the crime scene, it was already cordoned off. The victim, a young woman, lived in an apartment complex near the university. The building had a gray-shingled exterior and was on a quiet, dark side street. The forensics team had not yet arrived as Ren signed in. Before she stepped into the scene, she greeted Sean in the hallway.

"What's inside?"

"Young woman, dead in the bathtub. There are signs of blunt force at the back of her skull, and the floor of the bathroom is bloody."

"And how do we know it's a homicide?"

"We don't yet, but there is blood all over the bathroom floor, and there are some stains on the side of the tub. She can't have hit her head in this particular spot and ended up in the position she's in, mostly likely. Looks like the killer placed her in the tub to drain her."

"Any sign of forced entry?"

"No, but the girl's bedroom window is open. There is an external fire escape accessible from the window."

They were interrupted by the arrival of the forensics team, barreling up the stairs with their tackle boxes. Conlin grunted a hello, and his team isolated the bathroom and bedroom to collect evidence and take photographs. They allowed Ren and Sean entrance to the rest of the unit.

The detectives looked around the living room. It was sparsely furnished and yet strangely messy. There were bills at a desk, addressed to Ruby West at that address. A computer seemed to be missing from the desk, its absence noted by a fourteen- inch empty space amidst the mess of papers. They would bring the building manager downtown to ID the body; as it was, the crime scene was sealed to all but a few people.

Conlin joined them in the living room. "We've got the body in the bathroom. There are small animal prints in the blood in the bathroom and trailing it out to the bedroom window. Looks like a cat or small dog jumped out the window after the killing occurred."

The image of a terrified animal fleeing the scene made Ren ache a bit. She wasn't sure she could handle another case like this.

Moving into the kitchen, there were the remains of a holiday baking project. Wax paper was laid out on a table, with small chocolate truffles dried in place. They were dipped in crushed peppermint pieces. Another rack held small white cookies dusted in powdered sugar. There were dirty dishes on the stove and in the sink. There was a faint smell of something burnt. It looked as if the victim had spent some time baking that day. Sometime later, she was dead in her bathroom from blunt trauma to the head.

"The landlady found the body," Conlin told them. He was hovering around them in a way that irked Ren. "She said the fire alarm had been going off at strange intervals. She could hear it from her apartment. She found her at about six-thirty. I don't think the girl has been dead for long."

"The alarm was probably going off from this," Ren said, pointing to a batch of burnt cookies in the wastebasket. "So she's baking, the alarm is going off, and someone shows up and kills her. Then the landlady shows up."

"Sometimes fire alarms continue to go off long after something has burned," Sean said. He had lived in an apartment with a particularly sensitive system back in the Academy days.

"Looks like we've got a footprint on the carpet," Henry Wu said, leaning into the kitchen. Conlin left to investigate.

Ren opened a few elevated cupboards and then leaned down to peer into ones closer to the ground. Sean was looking at photographs on the refrigerator. A young woman, about twenty, was pictured at the beach with an older man and another young woman.

"I'll be damned," Ren said from her perch on the floor.

Sean glanced over to where she was crouching, and then walked over to join her. His partner had pulled something out of a low-lying cupboard. It was a brown box, with a receipt taped to the top. She was looking into the box, engrossed. As Sean got closer, he could see the box held a printout of some kind.

"What is it?" he asked her.

"A manuscript," she said.

Sean looked closer, not getting the significance. "So?"

"It was written by Lydia Merton," Ren said.

EVERYDAY ZION:
THE COMMUNITY AT SHADOW ROCK

A thesis by

Lydia Miranda Merton

Submitted to

Hester Lott, Coordinator

Verena Grau, First Reader

Harold Finnegan, Second Reader

Alternative religious communities in the US and elsewhere are hardly something new. In fact, a consensus of religious thinkers might well draw the conclusion that most religions are countercultural in nature. The mainline and evangelical forms of Christianity that exist in the US today draw their tradition from a history that is steeped in conflict. Traditional Christian theology developed in part in reaction against ruling elites in ancient Rome. Jesus, the leader of that movement, was killed for sedition against the government.[1]

And yet, newer religions always face greater scrutiny. There is a joke: "What is a religion?" The punch

---

1   Tyrone Barnes. Who Do You Say I Am? Roman Rule and the Contemporary World of Jesus of Nazareth. (New York: Pisces Press), 1988.

line is, "A cult plus a thousand years."[2] Communities like Shadow Rock, in Eplin, CA, might have a particular appreciation for such droll humor. Founded in 1980 after a series of visions by leader Tal Rasmussen, the community is now a self-sustaining farm with seven adult residents. The theology of Shadow Rock bears some resemblance to American Christian sects such as the Amish and the Shakers. There is no electricity or running water at Shadow Rock, and all of the food and clothing are produced by residents. Children, of which there are many at Shadow Rock, are educated by their parents.

However, there are significant ways that Shadow Rock differs from most modern religions in the US. The visions that led Tal Rasmussen to form the community are controversial and at times at odds with secular law. Although the community at Shadow Rock has never had any problems with the law, there are things that go on there that might be considered in violation of certain mainstream customs.

According to Rasmussen, he awoke one morning in 1980 to find a "being of light" at the end of his bed. It was a man, dressed in a white suit, emanating a soft and soothing light. He told Tal that he was a prophet, sent by God to ensure that Tal would make this vision a reality.

They walked for a while, in the desert lands behind Tal's house in Paradise Valley, AZ. The prophet told Tal about "3 Reversible Sins" that were causing society much harm. The first was usury. Tal, who worked as an insurance agent, knew that this was true. The

---

2 Attributed to George Carlin, citation unknown.

second sin was non-sustainable living. The third sin was misuse of the true nature of sexuality.

The being of light told Tal to "go home" and to live the way God originally intended. This would mean a life without usury, materialism, or recreational sexuality. He detailed to Tal a way of life that was simple and self-sustaining. He told him about the true nature of sexuality and the family.

After these events, Tal had a clear sense of what he needed to do. His family had owned land near Eplin, CA, for many generations. Tal sold all his earthly possessions and bought out the rest of his family to purchase a plot of 40 acres. He and his wife, Maude, with their two young children, moved onto the land in Eplin and built a small village. There was the family house, a schoolroom, and a dining hall. They planted crops and had a small collection of livestock.

Tal and Maude became artisans, making cheese, bread, and other provisions. Maude made wooden toys and dolls. Soon they were traveling part of the year to craft fairs and farmers markets. They traded their creations for needed items. No money ever exchanged hands; Tal and Maude were trying to live without it.

On these trips, Tal began to meet people that he invited to join the community at Shadow Rock. His pitch was evangelical in nature, and they had to agree with the theology before they were accepted. Tal believed that God was guiding him to the people who needed to be at Shadow Rock. It was all, he believed, for God's purposes.

Over the next two decades, many people came to Shadow Rock at Tal's invitation. Children were born. The residents were astonished at God's abundance.

With so little to sustain them, their lives were blessed beyond measure.

There were also those who left bitterly. Mary-Pat, a woman who works at the Blue Bell Café in Eplin, spent a summer there before leaving. "That place is full of kooks," she told me. "Tal is one slick cookie. His theology benefits him in ways that don't seem godly to me."

Another former resident, Jesse West, put it more succinctly: "Tal Rasmussen doesn't believe in God. He thinks he is God."

When asked to elaborate, West pointed to the quarterly tradition of fertility ceremonies. I will examine this controversial practice in chapter four.

The theology and customs of Shadow Rock will be the focus of this project. I had three weeks of up close contact with Tal and the current residents. I will examine their beliefs, their lifestyle, and the existence of these controversial fertility ceremonies.

What will emerge, I hope, is a portrait of an everyday Zion: an attempt at a return to paradise by people who are all too human.

CHAPTER EIGHTEEN

Lydia Merton finished reading and looked up. The detectives stared blankly at her. When they said nothing, and silence hung in the air between them, she resisted the impulse to make a joke. She knew better. She had already offered her alibi for the previous day when the girl had been killed: she had class in the afternoon and had picked up her car from the shop after work.

In the hour since she had arrived at the precinct, the detectives had shown her two websites, asked her several open-ended questions, and given her a copy of her manuscript. It was an alien artifact from a distant time in her life, and knowing that they had read it felt oddly violating. She was tempted, half-tempted, to ask for a lawyer.

"We've got three dead kids, Miss Merton," Ren said. "And they all seem to be connected to you."

Lydia squirmed in her chair. The detectives hadn't offered her anything to drink, and her throat was dry. She was bedraggled, having been awakened in the middle of the night by the detectives and a squad of cops. They had asked her to come in and told her that if she refused they would come back with a warrant. She had gone with them on the first request.

After another moment of awkward silence, Lydia spoke. "I'm sorry to hear about Ruby West. I only just met her. She stopped by my office a few weeks ago. She said she'd found my thesis online and wanted to talk about Shadow Rock. She'd grown up there."

"And you have spent time there, clearly."

"Yes, when I was in graduate school about eight years ago.

I was studying alternative religions at the GTU in Berkeley and heard about Tal Rasmussen. When it came time to do my thesis, I moved there for a few weeks, observed their rituals and customs, and wrote an ethnography." She tapped the manuscript in front of her. "And someone put it online. I don't know why. Ruby found my thesis and then found me. She was making a documentary about something that happened at Shadow Rock when she was a little girl."

"And she thought you might know something about it?"

"I guess so. But I don't know anything. I told her that. That's all the contact I've ever had with her."

"You didn't know her when you lived there eight years ago?"

"I don't remember her. She would have been a girl then, though, and I wasn't there for long. Maybe I did meet her once."

"Why would someone post your thesis online?"

"I have no idea. I didn't even finish the degree. My committee didn't like my findings and rejected my thesis. They said it lacked the essential ecumenical spirit that should accompany such research."

Ren and Sean stared at her blankly.

"In other words, I wasn't open-minded enough," she said. "When I first heard about Tal Rasmussen, Shadow Rock really spoke to me. They seemed to live this pure lifestyle. I was expecting something like the Amish. But I was disturbed by what I experienced there."

"How so?"

"I guess you haven't read chapter four yet. The fertility ceremonies."

They shook their heads.

"Tal claimed that he had experienced a vision. An angel told him about the true meaning of human sexuality. Sexual release was meant to be limited to certain times of the lunar calendar. He devised ceremonies that aligned with particular phases of the moon. The residents would have an outdoor ceremony on these designated dates, similar to a mass, and then.…"

"An orgy?" Sean asked.

"It was more straight-laced than that. Tal had sex with different women sequentially through the night, including the wives of others. The residents played drums in a circle while he did, usually under a full moon. I found it sleazy."

"You witnessed one of these ceremonies?"

"Yes. I was not asked to participate, but they let me observe it. I felt like I was on a porn set. So after that my research took a turn. I started to interview residents who'd left because they had had bad experiences. It got me into a bit of academic trouble because that wasn't what I signed up for."

"You quote Ruby's father in your introduction, Jesse West. What do you remember about him?"

Lydia thought for a moment. "Honestly, not all that much. I think I interviewed him by phone. One of the residents at Shadow Rock must have given me his name. Maybe his ex-wife, Ruby's mother."

The overhead lights blinked once. Ren got up, and a few seconds later Sean followed her out of the room. In the hallway, Lieutenant Roemer was waiting for them.

"The Subaru dealership confirmed that Lydia was there from six to seven tonight," she told them. "They've got a signed invoice and surveillance video of the waiting room. Pacific Community College confirmed she was in class from three to five. Conlin thinks Ruby West died late afternoon to early evening. I think Lydia's in the clear. The distance between the campus and the dealership alone eats up the hour between five and six."

The three stood for a few minutes, conferring in a huddle. Then the detectives returned to the interview room.

"You're free to go, Miss Merton," Ren said as she took a seat. "Please don't leave town without notifying us. And if you think of anything more that might be relevant to this case, let us know."

Lydia looked surprised, then relieved. The temperature in the room had cooled considerably since their last interaction. She stood up, feeling wobbly from nerves, and put her coat on. She left without saying another word to them.

There was something on her mind as she left the precinct, a thought so burdensome it could almost step out of her brain and walk around. She hadn't dared ask them, though, for fear of how it would look.

It was this: The detectives had mentioned three deaths that were connected to her. Lydia only knew of two.

• • •

Detective Sean Lukela approached the house with trepidation. Jesse West had just lost his only daughter, and it was nearing the holidays. Sean wanted to be respectful. He had not yet met Ruby's father. The medical examiner's office had handled the notification and arranged to have him ID his daughter's body.

Sean had several things on his mind today. He wanted to ask Ruby's father about her missing computer. They had found a website called shadowrock.net, which they believed Ruby had constructed. It had been disabled sometime before she died. The forensic team was doing its best to reconstruct the content, but that would take a while. If Jesse West knew what the website was about, that would save crucial time. Sean also needed the details of Ruby's life: her friends, boyfriends, how she spent her days. They would need to look into all of it.

There was also the matter of Jesse West and Shadow Rock

to consider. According to Lydia's thesis, Jesse had lived there and left bitterly. He had been quoted saying unkind things about the place, especially its leader, Tal Rasmussen. Religious types didn't always welcome dissidents. It was possible that Ruby's death was connected to the residents of Shadow Rock.

Jesse West's house was a modest structure, two-story. There were some wooden wind chimes tinkling in the wind and a padded swing on the front porch. There was a noticeable hole in the mesh that screened it in. Sean knocked on the door and waited. It was stony silent inside.

After a few moments he left the porch and walked around to the side. There was a Camry in the driveway and a small path leading to a backyard. A gate was open. Sean walked back, his hand on his weapon. When he got through the gate, he heard the sound of a chain rattling. It happened quickly: a dog barreled out of nowhere, barking in a loud and insistent growl. Sean jumped back. The chain stopped just a few feet short of where he was standing. The dog jumped up on two feet and pulled at the chain. He was howling.

Sean moved back to the street, cutting across the front lawn. He knocked again and waited for a moment, then pulled out his card and wrote a note to leave in the mailbox. This was always a crapshoot: sometimes people called back; sometimes they didn't. He would stop back again later as well. Sean hadn't gotten a court order, so things were still in the voluntary stage. He put the note in the mailbox and was turning around when he sensed someone standing in his peripheral vision.

"Are you here about the girl?" a voice said.

Sean turned fully around. A young woman, probably not seventeen, stood on the sidewalk. Her hair was French-braided, tied at the bottom by colored bubble fasteners. She had a blue halter-top on and a quilted, white down coat. She wore fringed moccasins that went up to her knees and a short, white skirt. His first thought was that she must be freezing cold in that getup.

"Pardon me, ma'am?" Sean asked.

"Are you here about the girl that died?"

"Which girl is that?"

"The girl on Capitol Hill. Cedar."

Sean stepped down onto the front sidewalk, nearer to her. They had not released Cedar's name to the media. This girl knew something.

"Do you know Jesse West?" he asked her.

She indicated that she did.

"Do you know when he'll be back?"

"I think he's inside," she said. "I don't think he wants to talk to you."

She walked past Sean, up onto the porch, and wiped her moccasins on the mat. When she pulled out a set of keys, he realized that she lived there.

"What is your name, ma'am?" he asked.

She unlocked the door, turning around to him for a moment before she disappeared inside.

"My name is Tal Rasmussen," she said.

CHAPTER NINETEEN

Ren looked at her reflection in the airplane window. She seemed to have aged a bit in the last two months. She felt haggard, tired. Outside, pitch black had given way to a grid of yellow light. The pilot had just told them to fasten their seatbelts for descent into San Francisco International Airport. Sean sat next to her, sleeping soundly. Neither of them had done much of that recently.

The decision to travel to Shadow Rock was a no-brainer, especially after they had time to read Lydia's thesis. If Lydia Merton had nothing to do with the girls' deaths, Shadow Rock was another possible link between them. Ruby had moved away with her father when she was ten, but had been compelled to set up a website about the place, which had been disabled the night she died. The forensics team was currently trying to reconstruct the content. Cedar died in Lydia Merton's house; Lydia had written a project about Shadow Rock. Cedar had also taken a trip to the Bay Area the spring before she died.

Ren took the thick manuscript from her tray table and shut the latch. She placed Lydia's thesis in her shoulder bag along side her laptop and cell phone. She had read most of it and felt somewhat prepared to visit Shadow Rock. Once they were on the ground, they would rent a car and drive the ninety minutes from SFO to Eplin.

Ren opened the case file, a thick collection of crime scene photos and reports. It was divided into three sections, the most recent first. Ren stared at a photo of Ruby. It was taken on a beach somewhere, not one she recognized. Sean had identified the girl in the photo with Ruby as Talia Rasmussen, Ruby's half-sister. He had met her the day before at Jesse's house in Ballard. She was the daughter of Ruby's mother and Tal Rasmussen.

Before they left Seattle, Ren had done a search for birth certificates naming Tallin Rasmussen as the father. There were seventeen in all, children ranging in age from one year to thirty-six. Only two were by his legal wife, Maude. Some of the names captivated her: Juniper, Salome, Jubilee. Tal Rasmussen had fathered a small nation, from the looks of it. And somehow Jesse West had ended up raising one of them in Seattle.

Ren was considering other connections between the dead girls. Ruby had voluntarily left her mother when she was ten years old, choosing a life with her father away from Shadow Rock. Cedar had left home as soon as her mother died. Both were runaways, in a sense. And yet they seemed to have different home lives.

All of this was rattling around in Ren's brain as they traveled to California. For the first time in years, she was thinking about her own origins and her feelings about them.

Ren had a photograph of Bebe and her father that she kept on her altar. They were standing on a red footbridge, with pink cherry blossom trees all around them. It was the only remnant she had of her parents' union and, much like the relationship itself, it was a bit enigmatic. Despite what the photo suggested, her parents had never been to Japan together. The image was captured at Golden Gate Park in San Francisco. They were on their honeymoon. In the photo, under her blue silk dress, Bebe was five months pregnant. Neil had thick Buddy Holly glasses and wore fur collars, both visible in the photo and in Ren's vague memories of him. She remembered walking with him one day in a lush park somewhere and watching manatees swim in an aqua blue tank. She couldn't remember ever exchanging a word with him. He had left when she was four.

Since that time, Ren had had no burning curiosity about her father. She had the tools at her disposal to find him but had never bothered to look. During dark moments with Del, Ren sometimes wondered if she had experienced an inconsolable loss when her father left, so buried within her that it only resurfaced in her choice of unstable women. But even at the most painful moments of her life, Ren still wasn't compelled to find Neil Jackson. He was her biological father, but Ren felt no strong pull to know him. She didn't even carry his name.

Ren understood what it was to grow up with a certain mystery about one's origins. She shared that in common with the dead girls. What she understood less was the desire they both seemed to have to know more about where they came from. If Ren could better understand this yearning, she thought she might be better able to understand why the girls had died. Their curiosity may have done them in. Something they had uncovered had been worth killing for.

• • •

Fat Elvis dreamt of ladyfingers. He dreamt of digits too wide to ever get a man's ring, with milk chocolate fingernails and a light dusting of powdered sugar. He awoke near the witching hour and scribbled something down, and then grabbed for it after the alarm went off at seven-thirty. As he lumbered out of bed, he examined the scrap of paper in the half-light of an Eplin dawn. *Dip the nails in crushed peppermint*, he had written.

Not a bad idea, he thought. He could make them for the cops from Seattle. He felt like baking for them. Having guests on Christmas was like having the Magi visit.

Jenny was awake, snug in a pink bathrobe, when he came out of the shower. She didn't look up. In front of her on the kitchen table were a half-dozen packages and four or five rolls of wrapping paper. There was coffee brewing on the stove.

"I'm thinking of making them veal loin tonight, maybe gingerbread for dessert," Fat Elvis said to her. "But I can't get this image out of my mind: ladyfingers, like the ones my mom used to make."

Jenny walked over and wrapped her arms around him. Her hair was a mess of tangled copper. She had gold rings on each of her fingers. She kissed his jowly cheeks.

"You think we have to time to fuck before the kid gets back?" she asked him. Their son was out doing his deliveries.

She stroked his midsection. His belly was rock solid, like bread dough that had sat in the fridge too long. He growled in response, burying his face in his wife's scent. She smelled of citrus and coffee beans. "No can do. I promised them breakfast at nine."

Jenny pulled away. "It's just as well. All Jonah needs is to find us humping in the kitchen on Christmas Eve morning."

Fat Elvis and Jenny lived in a guesthouse across a gravel parking lot from the Honeysuckle Inn, Eplin's only bed-and-breakfast. It was on the main drag near the highway exit, across from the high school and just a few blocks from the courthouse. Fat Elvis's great-grandfather, a burly Norwegian named Johannes Tuff, had built the house in 1903. It had flowerboxes outside the windows and a wrap around porch. Fat Elvis's parents had turned it into a bed-and-breakfast. He had run it since they died.

The detectives had arrived late the night before. They prepaid four nights and asked for directions to Rural Star route. They were polite but hadn't talked much. Fat Elvis had put the lady detective in the Arts and Crafts Room and the man down the hall in the room they called the Treehouse. They were to be their only guests.

He made his way across the lot, thinking of the cheese scramble and brown sugar bacon twists he would make for them. And then there were those ladyfingers. He could make them for teatime.

The entrance to the B&B was over the front porch through the kitchen. The design was a remnant of days when large families cooked and socialized together at home. Guests sometimes ate their breakfast on the porch, but it was too chilly for that today. The previous night he had set up the table near the stove for the detectives.

Fat Elvis let himself in. He pulled eggs and oranges out of the fridge. He had a yearning to serve the lady detective some fresh squeezed juice in her room, but thought better of it. He was a married man, after all.

By the time his bacon twists were sizzling, the detectives had joined him. They took their seats at the kitchen table. Both were engrossed in a file of reading material. After he served them, Fat Elvis left the kitchen for a smoke.

Ren surveyed the food platters in the center of the table. There were a dozen bacon twists and a mound of scrambled eggs with cheese. She stopped her brain from counting the calories. She selected one piece of bacon and a serving of eggs the size of a deck of cards.

Sean took a sip from his coffee. "Talia is living with Ruby's father. She must have left Shadow Rock with him when she was about eight." He was still processing his encounter with the girl two days before.

"I wasn't able to find anything online about a custodial agreement. Did she tell you anything?"

"No, those two don't seem to want to talk to us. But she knew Cedar's name, so clearly they know something." He thought for a second. "So Jesse West left Shadow Rock with his daughter and Tal's daughter. Who is their mother?"

Ren looked at the certificates more closely. "Tessa West."

"So Ruby and Talia are half-sisters. They have the same

mother. And Talia ends up living with her stepfather in Ballard. There must be a story there. Bad blood, maybe." Sean took another swig of coffee. "But it doesn't explain why Cedar ended up dead. Or Ruby. Or the boy downtown."

Ren continued to read her file, picking at her breakfast. Sean bit into a piece of bacon. It had a sweet taste, like caramelized sugar. He served himself a heaping portion of eggs and grabbed a few more bacon strips. Soon he was eating with gusto. He couldn't remember the last time he'd had food this good.

Ren got up and stretched. She had slept soundly in the arts and crafts bed, but not for long. "Why don't you join me outside when you're finished. I need a little fresh air."

Sean nodded, his mouth full of food.

"Must be nice to be able to eat like that," she said as she exited.

Ren left the kitchen and stood on the front porch. It was a wraparound that gave her a nearly 180-degree view of the property. Traffic was nonexistent on the street in front. Across the way there was a high school, also vacant for the holidays.

There were no phones or electricity at Shadow Rock, so she expected that some of the trip was going to be waiting around for interviews. They had talked to the Eplin sheriff before they left Seattle. He had notified Ruby West's mother of her death. She would have had time to process the news by the time they got there. Still, Ren knew they would be walking into a scene of guilt and grief. She expected that it would be a tough day.

A beige van turned off the main street and into the gravel driveway of the B&B. It was a VW bus. Its side was painted with an image of a large, pink honeysuckle bush. Ren watched as it parked near the guesthouse. A young man got out. He had shaggy black curls and a swimmer's body.

Ren peered back into the kitchen. Sean was still eating. She left the porch and crossed the lawn. The kid was loading stacks of braided bread into the van. Ren spotted sesame, saffron, and cinnamon. The loaves were in clear plastic bags fastened with twist ties. The bags were affixed with oval stickers with the same honeysuckle logo from the van.

Ren had done her research on the inn and its proprietors before they had booked their rooms. Fat Elvis's real name was Alvaro Ray. His family on his mother's side had long ties in Eplin, back to the turn of the twentieth century. Alvaro Ray had done an eighteen-month stint in his early twenties for marijuana possession. He was married to a woman named Jenny Fitch.

"You make all this stuff?" Ren said, smiling warmly. The kid returned the greeting. He was dressed in blue jean overalls and a thick lamb's wool sweater. He wore beige Crocs that matched the color of the van.

"My parents have it made. I'm just the distributor."

"Ever deliver to a place called the Blue Bell Café?"

"We did," he said. "Until they shut down a few years ago. Owners retired to Sedona. We sell mostly to grocery stores and cafes."

Ren was disappointed. She was hoping to track down a woman quoted in Lydia's thesis who worked there. "You don't know a woman named Mary-Pat, do you? Mid-forties probably? Worked there as a waitress."

"Can't say that I do," Jonah said, slamming the side door. "I don't mean to be rude, but I've got half my rounds still to do, and places are closing early today."

Ren pulled out a police sketch of Cedar and held it out to him. She would have to be quick about this. It was the same image that was all over Seattle and the news. They had reconstructed her face from the crime scene photos. They had not released her name to the public. "Can you tell me if you've ever seen this girl?"

He looked at the sketch, then folded it up and handed it back to her.

"Cedar," he said. "She was here last spring."

CHAPTER TWENTY

Shadow Rock was three miles out on Rural Star Route. Ren drove, tapping her fingers on the steering wheel. She had never been to Northern California before, and it looked different today in the daylight. Everything seemed yellow compared to the lush green of Seattle. The hills surrounding Eplin were the color of dry mustard. Cypress lined the route. She could smell eucalyptus on the morning breeze. Sean had his window cracked. He was feeling a little carsick.

"My first interview, and I've already got a bite. He knew Cedar's name, Sean." She had let Jonah return to his rounds with the promise that they would talk more later. "I'm thinking police work is pretty easy in small towns."

"Don't get cocky just yet," Sean replied. "I'm placing even odds no one at the village recognizes the sketch."

Ren spotted the mailboxes. Fat Elvis had told her to look out for them. One was covered with monarch butterflies and ladybugs. Another had sunflowers. She turned off the highway and drove up a gravel road. They crested a hill. Yellow fields were all around, all denuded at this time of year. Ren could picture corn stalks and blackberry thickets in the summer, and fruit hanging heavily from the trees in the orchard. There were animals—chickens and goats behind wire fences. In a distant field, two horses grazed.

Shadow Rock was a tiny village—four houses built around a well. There were two outdoor showers. It had been named for its literal location: it was in the shadow of a hill that had three large rocks looming at the top.

As they crossed into the property, there was a small,

wooden bridge. A rushing creek ran below it. Ren drove the car over the bridge and parked. She and Sean got out. There was a reverent stillness all around. As they walked, Ren noticed that there was no cell service.

A girl, aged about four, stood with her dolly near the well. Her hair was a toe-headed rats' nest. When they got a better look, they realized that the girl was a boy. It was hard to tell. He was wearing a smock that looked like a dress. Before they could say anything, he ran off.

"That might be Nazareth," Ren said to Sean. "His mother is a woman named Uriah. I swear I am not making that up." She had looked at the birth certificates so many times she felt like she knew the kids.

Ren looked around, noticing that one structure had open holes where the windows should be. The door was also wide open. When she approached she saw it was some kind of smoke house: a single room with several wood-burning ovens. There were herbs drying on racks and a small, adjacent room that smelled of jerky.

A woman in a peasant top and floor length skirt, her hair wrapped in a kerchief, was kneading dough as Ren entered. She looked up, unsmiling.

Instantly, Ren knew: it was Ruby's mother. They had the same facial features and hazel eyes. Ruby's image in photographs had burned onto Ren's brain. Now watching this older version in live action, she felt a chill dread.

Two other women were gathered around her. They held babies that were so similar they could have been twins, although the mothers were a study in contrasts. One had flaming red Medusa hair, and the other had black plaits like Sacagawea.

"Mrs. West," Ren said to the kerchiefed woman. "I know this is a difficult time for you. My partner and I just have a few questions."

She looked at Ren penetratingly. Saying nothing, she turned around and placed some bread dough on a rack in the fire pit. Then she swatted at something in midair and left the room.

Sean stood with the women and their look-alike babies. Ten blinking eyes stared at Ren.

"Do you know where she went?" Ren asked them. "Is she coming back?"

"I think she went up to the rocks," Medusa said. "She's been up there a lot recently."

From the looks of it, the rocks were a good two miles away from the property, amidst steep terrain. It was hard to imagine a woman in a long skirt scaling the hill. Ren knew from reading Lydia's thesis that that was where they held the fertility ceremonies.

"Maybe one of you can take me up there?" Ren asked.

The women shook their heads in tandem. They were starting to remind Ren of geisha girls. "It's a sacred place," Sacagawea said. "You have to be one of us."

Ren pulled out the sketch of Cedar and showed it to them. "Does this person look familiar to you?" she asked.

They viewed the image and then looked at each other. They shook their heads.

Ren was starting to get annoyed. Sean seemed strangely absent to her, standing next to them in compliant silence. Perhaps he was having a call to Jesus moment, or maybe just some girl-on-girl fantasy. "How about Tal? Is he here?" Ren asked.

The women shook their heads. "Tal and Maude are traveling with the artisan markets this month. They're due back tomorrow."

"They're not coming back tonight?" Ren asked. "It is a religious holiday, isn't it?"

The women looked puzzled. Then one of them said,

"Christmas is the Prophet's birthday. In our tradition we don't celebrate birthdays."

• • •

Christmas morning Lydia Merton woke up alone. This wasn't unusual, as she had done little to celebrate the holidays since her parents died twelve years ago. She had a cousin in Charleston and another in San Francisco, but they weren't the types to make an effort. Their cards were on her hearth, above a rope of evergreen boughs she had hung above her fireplace.

The house was quiet as she ground her coffee beans. She could hear neighbors piling up their cars, slamming trunks filled with gifts and shouting greetings to people across the way. In the distance a choir at Holy Names sang of ransom captive Israel.

It was a holiday, but in some ways it was just a typical morning. Lydia's life was a solitary one. It had not always been like this. Lydia had had friends once: women who gathered once a month to discuss books and update each other about their lives. She had even gone to Mexico with a group of them. She had a picture of three of them wearing straw hats and holding an enormous iguana. They were drunk on margaritas and burned red from jet skiing.

She could remember that trip vividly, but her life as a friend seemed distant to her now. Women were like strange, exotic cities. Lydia preferred the familiar cloister of her own thoughts.

Lydia checked her messages reflexively as she spread some marmalade on her wheat toast. No word from David. She wasn't expecting to hear from him. Christmas was the one day he wouldn't dare. He did have his rules.

Lydia showered and changed into her running clothes. She was an inconsistent exerciser, doing a three-mile loop a few times a month. She didn't need to do it, so she didn't have much incentive. Rail-thin women were the norm in the Merton family.

Today was a good day for it, though. It was brisk and bright as she set out. The sidewalks were empty. She kept pace as she left Capitol Hill and entered the trail when she reached Interlaken. Huge trees towered overhead, creating a canopy of dark. She took the cement road until she reached a dirt trail and then headed up a peaty incline.

Her heart was steady, beating in her ear. She felt some pain but pushed her way through it. It was a half-mile to a clearing. She focused on a spot of sunlight at the crest ahead of her.

When she reached the top, she stopped, checking her heart rate near her ear. Below her, Montlake gave way to the University District. She spotted the ship canal in the foreground and Husky Stadium farther on. Her parents had met at a game there in the sixties. He was the head of the campus Republicans, whose twin was pledging Gamma Phi Beta. She set him up with one of her sorority girls, a pretty blonde from Iowa City.

They met for the first time at a Huskies-Redwings game. Lydia's mother had a knee-jerk revulsion to his buzz cut and the vest he was wearing. They sat a foot apart in the bleachers and didn't talk much. A blustery wind picked up, and he offered her his flannel blanket. She looked over at him and just like that, it was love. They married three months later and were together until the day she died.

Lydia had heard the story many times. She had told it at funerals and weddings. Love was something you stumbled into. Sometimes it lasted for a long time. It had for her parents.

Lydia inhaled deeply, taking in the pine and the sea salt. She thought of David, walking ahead of her on the trail at Lake Louise. They had hiked for miles, until their breath was raggedy and their kneecaps ached. She recalled the blanket of stars overhead at night, as they lay side-by-side under a sky-light in their room. She thought of that last morning, as she stood outside the Deer Lodge while David pulled the rental car around. She had closed her eyes and made a wish.

May it ever be so.

Her mother used to say that, and Lydia liked its simplicity. It had been Lydia's wish that last day at Deer Lodge to always be in love with David and to always have times like this with him. She knew the odds were against them, both because of his vocation and because of the fleeting nature of love. But so far they were making it. Even the option of other men wasn't dampening their bond. She believed that they had the kind of enduring connection that her parents had. What better gift could she have on Christmas? She closed her eyes and thanked God for what she had.

Lydia turned around and began to descend the slope back into the park. She would pick up the pace in a minute. For now she was enjoying the moment. It was Christmas Day and she was alone, but she was happy.

She walked, lost in thought. As the trail turned, she noticed someone in the distance. A figure moved at a quick clip, coming up the same trail. A race-walker, was Lydia's first thought. She averted her eyes, the code of exercisers everywhere.

As they moved closer together, Lydia looked again. A thought fluttered: *I know you.* She was unsure, and looked again, more intently. She smiled expectantly, forming a greeting.

Everything went black as Lydia took the force of the blow.

CHAPTER TWENTY-ONE

Ren tapped on the door to the Treehouse, a little more intently the second time. It was nearly noon on Christmas Day, and Sean hadn't been at breakfast. Ren had made small talk with Fat Elvis while she drank hot chocolate and ate saffron bread. It was shaped like a wreath and had almond slivers on top.

Jenny had left them a small, wrapped gift outside their rooms. Ren had opened hers: a beaded bracelet. It was rattling on her wrist now as she knocked.

When the door opened, Ren almost gasped. Her partner stood there in his blue-striped pajama bottoms and white wife beater. His hair was ruffled, and his face was wan.

"God, what happened to you?"

"Bacon twists," he croaked, moving back to the bed. He crawled back under the covers. "I think I have food poisoning."

Ren cleared his clothes off the armchair and took a seat. She glanced at Sean's phone on the nightstand. There were two messages from Lieutenant Roemer. Ren had not yet brought up with her partner the rumor she'd heard about him from Stella Hadley. Had he possibly turned in his resignation?

"I was up all night. I'm surprised you didn't hear me."

Ren was grateful for the distance between the Arts and Crafts Room and the Treehouse. She had slept soundly, lulled by the scent of eucalyptus outside her window and the huge moon overhead.

"Did you hear the coyotes howling last night?"

"No, I slept right through that," she said. "Are you sure you're really sick?"

Sean shot open an eyelid from underneath his quilt.

"Sorry. You know what I mean. I guess this explains why you were being so weird yesterday."

"What do you mean?"

"I could have used a little support with those freaky geisha women."

Sean opened both eyes this time. "I was trying not to vomit all over those two cute babies."

Ren laughed. "It's not just that. You seem almost checked out these days. Is there something on your mind?"

Sean said nothing.

"Tal is supposed to be back today. I'm ready to head out there. This is a big deal."

"You see there? Yesterday was good prep for you."

"I'm just sorry you're going to miss out on the show." She set the wrapped gift on the nightstand. "What did the lieutenant want?"

Sean opened his eye again. "What?"

Ren motioned to his phone.

"Oh, she was just checking in. She has some concerns about Bridge Heekin and decided to subpoena his phone records. She wants to be able to completely clear him."

As Ren got up to leave, Sean said, "There is something else I've been meaning to tell you. You might want to sit down again."

Ren did as she was told.

"You remember the Christmas party last year?"

Ren nodded. She had had a few sloe gin fizzes and danced to the ragtime band.

"I had a few too many, so when it came time to leave, Lieutenant Roemer offered to give me a ride home," Sean said.

"We were out near Skyway when we got pulled over. The lieutenant blew the sobriety test by just a point."

Ren was shocked. Lieutenant Roemer seemed so responsible. She should have known better.

"It was bogus, but the arresting officer was in training and trying to impress his boss. There was no way we could get out of it. We got pulled into Seattle South. The booking officer at the precinct was a buddy of mine, so I was able keep it from going any further. I felt so bad. It was my fault she was out that way, and she was barely a dot over the line. If it had been anyone else, they would have turned a blind eye."

Ren had a sinking feeling what was coming next.

"I thought it had all gone away, but somehow Conlin found out about it. I don't know how. So I wanted to tell you that I think we all need to prepare for the inevitability. He's talking about launching an investigation. He could get both me and the lieutenant fired for this. You know he wants to be in charge. This is his ticket in."

Ren was waiting for Sean to tell her about the job interview he'd been on, but he said nothing.

"Thank you for telling me," Ren said. She touched his arm as she left the room. She would miss him today. She wasn't willing to consider that this might be their last case together.

• • •

It took about ten minutes to get from the Honeysuckle Inn to Shadow Rock. Ren spotted the rocks in the distance, bathed in sunlight. She had read about the area in Lydia's thesis. The residents hiked up to a clearing four times a year, built a bonfire, and held a blessing ceremony. In keeping with the theology of the place, this was officially the only way children were conceived at Shadow Rock.

When Ren turned off the main road and passed over the

bridge, she saw a flatbed truck that hadn't been there the previous day. Her heart began to race. She checked her Glock in its holster as she got out of her car.

Lydia had described Tal Rasmussen in her manuscript as intense and incoherent. After the previous day, Ren had a better idea of what she meant. Shadow Rock had a rhythm that was out of step with the contemporary world. The land was preternaturally quiet, as if it had absorbed the contemplative nature of its residents. It seemed to be a place absent of craven desires.

Ren entered the village. No one seemed to be around. She walked over to the smoke house where she had found Tessa West yesterday. The door was open. A large table inside was covered with all kinds of items: glass jars of honey, stacks of dried herbs, metal vats of oil. Ren looked around the space, which was empty. A wood stove was burning, showing a small pile of glowing embers.

"I've been expecting you," a man said.

Ren jumped. She turned to the area where she had heard the voice. A man was sitting in a corner. He was slight, barely five foot five. He had a beatific countenance and a voice that barely rose above a whisper. He had raven black hair framed by curls at the tips. "You're the lady detective, aren't you?" he said. He hadn't moved from his chair.

"I'm Detective Copeland," Ren said. She had her hand on her gun.

"Tal Rasmussen," the man said, standing up. When he walked over, she realized why he had been sitting: he had a noticeable limp. "Sorry if I startled you. I can't stand for long. Maude and I are just back this morning, as you can see. Sorry I wasn't here to greet you yesterday."

Tal looked around expectantly. "I was told there would be two of you," he said.

"My partner is under the weather. Food poisoning, perhaps."

"Oh, I've got something for that," Tal said. He dug around on the table before handing her a blue ceramic cork-stoppered bottle. "Brew it like tea."

Ren accepted the gift. She wouldn't give it to Sean. No cop would dare drink something from a suspect.

"Ren Copeland," Tal said, taking a seat at the table. "I guess that explains why you're working on the Prophet's birthday. I have great respect for the chosen tribes."

Ren took a seat across from him. "How long have you been on the road?"

"About four weeks," Tal said. "It's all I can handle with my bum leg. Maude does most of the driving."

"You make a living at farmers' markets?"

"In a matter of speaking. We trade. We only exchange money when there is no alternative."

"Where were the markets?"

"We were up and down California this trip."

"Sounds like a lot of work."

Tal had gotten up again. He filled a teakettle with water from a pump. Then he placed it on a grill in the wood-burning oven.

"I am sorry for your loss, Mr. Rasmussen. Ruby was here for most of her childhood. This must be a blow to you."

"She is with God now," he said.

"She was so young."

He nodded. "Some lilies live only for a day. It's not for us to judge."

The teakettle began whistling. Tal got up and poured a mug of hot water and added a teabag. A scent of lavender filled the room. "Energy is neither created nor destroyed," he said. "Ruby has changed her earthly form. I'd like to think she might visit us here again." He took a sip of tea and looked deeply at Ren, long enough that she started to feel uncomfortable. Finally he said, "What do you believe in, detective?"

"I don't practice a religion," she said. Before the worst of it with Del she had, but not since then. She had faith in nothing.

"Everyone believes in something."

She considered that for a moment. "I believe that no one should get away with murder. Ruby was brutally attacked. Another woman was too."

"*Tikkun olam*," Tal said. "It is your job to heal a broken world."

"To do my part, yes. You can help me if you have any information."

"Some philosophies might tell you otherwise: that it is a person's destiny to kill and remain undiscovered. We're just players in a larger story."

Ren was beginning to understand Lydia Merton in whole new ways. How could Tal be so detached in the face of murder and death? She couldn't imagine spending three weeks at Shadow Rock.

She pulled out the sketch of Cedar. "Do you recognize this girl?"

Tal looked at it for a moment. "She died too?"

Ren nodded.

Tal handed the sketch back to her. "She doesn't look familiar to me."

"Mr. Rasmussen, I need to ask you something. I hope you understand I am not meaning to embarrass you. You had a daughter with Tessa. She left Shadow Rock with Jesse West."

"Many of my children have left. Only three are here now. My tribe is moving out into the world. They have their destinies to fulfill."

"Yes, but Talia left at a young age. That must have been painful for you."

Tal's face clouded over. He gave Ren the once-over. The room was deathly quiet.

"Sir, are you still angry at Jesse West for taking away your child?"

Tal got up from the table. He waved his hand in the air—a movement similar to the one Tessa had made yesterday—and left the room. Ren sat there for a moment longer. The fire in the stove crackled and spit. In the distance, she heard horses whinnying.

Ren left the smoke house and looked up at the rocks in the distance. Tessa had gone up there yesterday. She could just make out a snake of a trail leading from the property to the base of the hill.

As she left the village, Ren turned right and drove for a bit. She was looking for a side road that might lead up to the rocks. After about a half-mile, there was a gravel turnoff. She took a right and drove up for a bit, until she reached a green metal gate. It was locked. She got out of the car. In the distance she could see the three large rocks that topped the hill. There didn't seem to be any public way to access the area. No one at the village seemed to want to let her on the land. If she broke onto the property, anything she found would be inadmissible.

Luckily, she had another idea.

• • •

Ren drove back to Eplin with one thing on her mind. She needed to talk to Jonah again. Chances were good he would be at home. It was the benefit of the holiday. She had to get him on record about the things he'd told her. He was a witness placing Cedar in Eplin before her death. The residents of Shadow Rock were denying ever having met her. It was something.

Ren reached over and touched the stoppered bottle that Tal had given her. She pulled out the cork and sniffed it suspiciously. A musty odor like dried mushrooms tickled her nose. "Drink it like tea," Tal had said. She would send it to the lab, just to be sure.

Eplin was quiet as Ren turned off Rural Star Route. There were few cars as she took the main thoroughfare back to the inn. On either side as she drove there were colonials and Victorians and occasionally a Craftsman bungalow. Oak trees lined the way, as stately as uniformed men.

As she neared town, a flash of turquoise caught her eye. She looked in the direction it came from but it had disappeared behind an oak. A moment later she saw it again.

As she got closer, Ren saw that it was a woman draped in a turquoise sari. Her hair was pulled up off her face. She was moving at a leisurely pace, looking up and around her as she went.

Ren turned into a 76 station when she came to it. She filled the tank and bought a coffee and a cookie wrapped in cellophane. It had the Honeysuckle Inn stamp. Apparently they sold cookies as well. Ren felt that she had earned the splurge. It was Sunday, after all.

The beanpole ringing her up had a bushy moustache and a shark's tooth around his neck on a leather string. He was wearing red flannel and had a tattoo around his wrist.

"Do you know a woman around here who dresses in a sari?" Ren asked. The kid looked at her quizzically. She wondered if she should explain what a sari was. Maybe he misheard her.

"The Taj Mahal," he said after a moment. "Maybe a waitress from the Taj Mahal in Castro."

Ren had noticed references to Castro. There was a binder in her room at the inn about local attractions. Castro seemed to have all the ethnic food. Ren had spotted Thai, sushi, and a German bakery in the listings. Evidently there was Indian as well.

"They open over the holidays?" she asked him, and he shrugged. "Most things will open back up tomorrow," he said.

Ren gave the kid a closer look. He was about Jonah's age. They might have been friends in high school. "Have you ever been out to the rocks?" she asked him.

He shook his head, and again when she showed him the sketch. When she left, Ren caught a glimpse of him checking her out. She was beginning to think that dating might be a lot easier in small towns too.

Driving back from the 76, Ren called her mother. Bebe picked up on the first ring.

"Honey, I've been so worried about you. I was remembering this episode I saw of *20/20*. There was this man who claimed to be the reincarnation of Jesus, but really he was molesting kids."

Now was not the time to tell Bebe that she was doing the investigation alone. Ren unwrapped the cookie and bit into it. It was peanut butter dipped in milk chocolate, still fresh. "Everything's OK here, Mom. It's a charming, small town. I'm making progress."

"Well, your brother and I miss you. We're having a party at Sanctuary for New Year's. The band is going to be there."

Ren shook her head. They would never give up on this. Ren and the Drummer was their year-end project. "I'm not interested in meeting RJ, Mom. I think I like someone else."

Bebe clucked. "Please tell me you're not talking about that dreadful girl." This was Bebe's name for Delphine. "I've seen you fall into that abyss one too many times."

"I'm living abyss-free these days, Mom," Ren said. "And this is my turnoff. We'll talk later." She hung up the phone. The van was not in the parking lot as Ren pulled in. She walked over to the guesthouse. The door was shut tight. She knocked loudly.

Jonah answered. He was dressed in khaki overalls without a shirt.

"I thought you might be gone," Ren said. "Where is the van?"

"My parents took it. They're over at the Iron Horse."

Ren surmised that something other than the 76 station was open on Christmas. "I wanted to talk to you more. I'm also wondering if you've ever been up to the three rocks on the hill overlooking the village."

Jonah nodded. "Yeah, I took Cedar there. She wanted to see it. There is an old road off Rural Star that goes up that way. The direct route has a locked gate, but there is one other way."

"You think you could show me how to get there?" Ren asked. She knew the residents would be no help. This was her best shot at seeing the area.

Jonah nodded. He disappeared inside and emerged wearing the same heavy sweater made of lamb's wool that he had worn the previous day.

Ren had decided on this plan on the way home. She wanted to see the rocks, and she needed to interview Jonah. She also would feel better having someone with her. She had her gun if anything got out of hand, but two were better than one.

"Tell me more about your encounter with Cedar," Ren asked him as they got into her car. The stoppered bottle was sitting on the seat. He picked it up and held it in his hands as they left the driveway.

"I met her in town, when I was doing my deliveries. She

had come by Greyhound bus. We got to talking. She said she had grown up knowing that she was born in Eplin, and she was curious about it. When her mother died, she decided to come and have a look. I told her some of what I knew, and I took her to the rocks. She believed she was conceived in one of the ceremonies." He removed the cork from the bottle and sniffed.

"You can just toss that into the glove compartment," Ren said.

Jonah opened the box and placed it next to a set of handcuffs. "Yeah, we went out to the rocks together, and then I drove her to the village. I don't know how she got back; someone must have given her a ride. I saw her the next afternoon. She said she'd gotten some information that was helpful to her."

They had reached the mailboxes near the village. Ren kept driving Rural Star Route about a half-mile. The gravel road was on the right. She could see the green gate locked up the way.

"Keep going," Jonah said. "It's another half-mile or so."

She kept driving until they crossed a small stone bridge. After it, there was a grassy turnoff that led up to a rocky incline.

"I should have warned you. This is a dangerous road. No one uses it anymore."

Ren shifted gears and headed up the hill. A steep ravine with a rushing creek ran below and to the right. This must have been the body of water that also ran through the village.

After about a mile and a half of rough terrain, they came to a clearing. "We can hike in from here," Jonah said, unbuckling his seat belt.

When they got out of the car, a chill wind had picked

up. Ahead of them at a distance were the three jagged rocks, emerging from the earth like giants. The sun peered through clouds overhead.

It was about a half mile on foot. They walked through the bramble and sage grass, keeping the rocks in view.

As they got nearer, Ren saw a circle of stones encapsulating a fire pit. She could envision a group of people here, surrounding the flames. She imagined their drums and a full moon overhead.

She was also trying to imagine what would compel a seventeen-year-old to come here. "Was she curious about meeting Tal? She thought he was her father?"

"I think that was part of it. But there was something more as well. She said she had grown up with this gut feeling that the woman raising her was not her biological mother."

So Cedar's curiosity about her origins went a little deeper than they had thought. It made sense. Losing her mother might have kicked the desire for answers into overdrive.

"Did you have a romantic relationship with Cedar?" Ren asked him. "You spent some time together."

Jonah laughed. "God no."

"What do you mean? It's a reasonable question."

Jonah moved past Ren. He walked through the clearing, past the stone circle, and over to one of the big rocks. Ren pulled her sweater around her. She walked over to join him. In the distance she could see Shadow Rock village, which looked tiny. She could see a smoke stack rising from the main house and could spot the serpentine creek bed.

Jonah was dwarfed by the immensity of the rocks, but his next words filled the space between them. "I wasn't just helping Cedar out of the kindness of my heart. I think I was born here too."

CHAPTER TWENTY-TWO

"You think you were conceived in one of the ceremonies here?" Ren asked. She flashed on an image of Jenny. Ren had seen her around the inn but had only gotten a sense of her. Could she have lived at Shadow Rock once?

Jonah nodded his head. "When Cedar told her story, about growing up with these weird feelings about her mother, I could totally relate. I have this memory of being near these rocks when I was a little boy. I was with some woman, but I don't think it was my mother. It's all so hazy to me that I'm not even sure it wasn't some dream I had. But when I met Cedar and she talked about the same thing, it got me curious."

Ren was putting it all together. If Cedar and Jonah were both conceived here, their biological father was Tal Rasmussen. They would have been half-siblings. That's why Jonah had laughed at her suggestion of a romance. The question was, who had birthed these two kids and what happened to her? Could this be why the residents at Shadow Rock were denying having met Cedar? Could it be why Cedar was killed? And Ruby? And the boy found downtown?

"Did you talk about the fact that you might be siblings?"

"God no," Jonah said. "I had just met her. She wasn't here for long. I took her to the Greyhound station a few days after I met her."

"What was her frame of mind when she left? Had she gotten any answers?"

"She seemed to think so. She had met someone at the village, and they gave her the name of someone in Seattle who could help her."

"Who was it?"

"The name they gave her? I'm not sure. She lived in Seattle though. Cedar was going to look her up when she got back."

Ren could imagine it all now. Cedar traveled to Eplin after her mother died the previous spring. She wanted to find out how she had made it into the world. Whatever she had found led her to Lydia Merton. "Jonah, I need you to think about this. What was the name they gave her?"

Jonah hung his head. He was looking at the village below. "I don't think she ever told me."

The wind had picked up again. The sun was shifting lower in the sky. It was getting colder. Ren was looking forward to being back in the toasty Arts and Crafts Room. She couldn't wait to get into a hot bath. She had a lot to mull over.

Lydia Merton's house was targeted by Cedar, she was certain of that now. Whatever it was Cedar was looking to find, it was bad enough that the residents of Shadow Rock were denying having met her when she came to Eplin, and it was bad enough that someone in Seattle had been willing to kill over it. Then there was Ruby. She had set up a website about Shadow Rock, which had been disabled the day she died. Whatever she knew may have gotten her killed.

"Should I be worried?" Jonah asked. His face seemed open, innocent. "It sounds like someone is killing off my contemporaries."

"I don't think so, Jonah," Ren said. "You've been helpful today. I appreciate you giving up your holiday for this."

He smiled at her. "No problem."

They stayed like that a moment longer. When Ren turned to leave, she felt him move in closer to her. When she looked up at him, she realized he was going in for a kiss.

Ren strong-armed him with a stern look, and his face changed. "I'm sorry," he said. "You were just so pretty standing there. There is something about you that I find compelling."

Ren moved quickly away from him. She was feeling utterly disarmed. How had Jonah misread this situation? Surely he knew he had just compromised the case by doing that?

When she got to the car, she turned around. She had been so lost in thought that she hadn't noticed that Jonah wasn't behind her. She retraced her steps, emerging on the other side of one of the big rocks. She looked to both sides. There was nothing on either side. Jonah was not there.

In the distance she saw someone walking in the village. It was a stick figure dressed in white. She saw three women. They were walking together. She thought she heard children playing in the distance. It was hard to say, though: it may have been the rushing creek.

That was the last thing she remembered before she blacked out.

● ● ●

When Ren awoke, she smelled wood smoke. It was strangely comforting in the darkness. Her head was throbbing, and she could taste metal. She felt beneath her for the soft grass. She sat up. When she looked behind her she could see the three solitary rocks in the distance.

She didn't remember fainting, but it was clearer to her now. She had rolled down the hill a bit. It would be a steep climb to get back up. She was freezing cold, so much so that she didn't want to move. She wanted to huddle for warmth until the sun came up.

Before she passed out, she had seen a figure in white walking in Shadow Rock village. Was that Jonah she saw? She was starting to think her mind was playing tricks on her. Was it possible Jonah had hit her from behind? She couldn't recall that. She remembered standing at the car and walking back to the rocks alone.

Ren forced herself to stand up. She knew she had to get moving to warm up. She took a few tentative steps up the incline toward the rocks. She reached in her pocket for her phone. There was no service, but the clock read 5:08. She had been knocked out for over fourteen hours.

Ren used the light from the phone to look around the incline near her. She could see a few feet in any direction. The battery was running low. She shut down her phone.

She was alone out here. Jonah was gone. He must have been the one to attack her. She had been foolish to trust him. She knew that now.

As she moved up the incline, she heard a noise. At first she thought it was the wind. It was as low moan, but she thought it was saying her name.

Ren. Ren.

She looked behind her. She could sense the slope beneath her feet, but it was too dark to see far. She stood there for a moment, seeing only black. Then white in the distance as it moved toward her. She heard the noise again.

Ren Ren.

It was a woman's voice, she realized, coming from somewhere down the slope. Ren could just make out the white of her clothing. The white was moving closer to her. It was moving up the hill toward her.

Ren pulled her gun. "Don't come near me," she screamed into the air. "I have a gun, and I will use it."

She could see the white, now stopped in place.

"I'm not going to hurt you," the woman said. "I saw a light flashing up there. I thought I was alone out here."

Ren held her gun firmly in place. She was taking no chances. "You may approach slowly. My gun is aimed at you."

The woman came closer. She was in a long, white dress and heavy, white lamb's wool sweater similar to the one Jonah had been wearing the day before.

"Usually when I encounter something out here at this time of the morning, it's a coyote," she said. "But with your gun you might be even more scary."

Ren could feel blood trickling down her forehead. She had a gash somewhere above her hairline.

"I don't think we've met. I'm Maude Rasmussen," the woman said. "Looks like you took a beating last night."

Ren was still getting her bearings. She remembered being at the car and then walking back to the rocks. She had seen a figure in the village in the distance. She couldn't be sure now what she had really seen. That was the last thing she recalled before she blacked out. And now, standing here with Maude, she wasn't sure what she had heard. Was that Maude calling her name just now? Or had she imagined it?

"If you'd like you can come back to the smoke house," Maude said. "I can fix you some tea. Everyone's asleep."

"I've got my car," Ren said. It was a good mile away, through the heavy brush. It would be hard to get to it before sunrise.

"I can drive you up there to get it. At the least you should get some water and a bandage before you get behind the wheel."

Ren was in no mood to take chances, but the woman had a point. "How far is it to the village?"

"A half a mile, I'd say. What were you doing up there, anyway?"

"I was having a look around," Ren said. "I was with Jonah Ray."

Maude gave her a knowing look. "Well, that explains it," she said.

• • •

By the time they got back to the smoke house, Ren was feeling a little bit more like herself. The walk had warmed her, and she was less disoriented. Maude built a fire in the wood-burning stove and pumped some water into a glass.

Ren drank the water greedily. She was parched. Maude filled a kettle and placed it on a grill in the stove. When it began to whistle, she poured hot water into a bowl, and then pumped some cold water into it. She walked over and began washing Ren's forehead.

"How well do you know Jonah?" Ren asked her.

"Eplin's a small town. We all know each other a bit."

Maude dried Ren's forehead and patted her hair with a towel. She took some astringent and rubbed it into Ren's wounds. Ren winced and bit on a towel to swallow the pain. The room fell quiet as Maude bandaged Ren's head.

When she was done, Maude washed her hands and placed the kettle back into the fire. After it reheated, she fixed two cups of tea and placed one near Ren.

"What did you mean when you said that my being with Jonah explained what happened up there?" Ren asked.

Maude took a sip of tea. "Jonah started to cause some trouble for us a few years ago. Some of the residents would find him up near the rocks, loitering about with girls from town. That is a sacred place for us, and he was using it like lovers' lane."

"He had sex up there?"

"Yes, that was my understanding. Took girls from town up there and had his way with them. You have to hand it to him. He was going the extra mile to impress them. When Tal found out, he had a talking to him. I thought it had stopped."

Ren's mind was fuzzy. Had Jonah assaulted her? She wasn't sure now. She remembered him leaning in for a kiss. He seemed contrite when she rebuffed him. But why had she collapsed up there? Had he hit her from behind? And where was he now?

"I wanted to ask you something," Ren said. She was hoping she'd have better luck with Maude than she had with Tal. She pulled out the sketch of Cedar. "Have you ever met this girl?"

Ren looked at Maude sharply as she took the sketch from her. She was hoping for any glimmer of recognition.

Maude shook her head.

Ren's mind was beginning to reel. Was it possible Jonah had made up the story about Cedar? He had known her name, though, which hadn't been released to the media. That was why she trusted him. Talking to Maude now, she felt confused. One of them was lying to her.

Ren took a sip of tea. She could taste a hint of toasted rice. She wouldn't normally drink anything from a suspect, but hydration was a concern. "Why is it that Tal and Tessa's daughter lives in Seattle with Jesse West?"

Maude got up and pulled a loaf of bread from a cooling rack. She tore it in half and offered some to Ren. Ren shook her head and waited.

Finally, Maude spoke. "When Talia was eight and Jesse and Ruby were leaving, she insisted on going with them. Tal was on the road so much that I think she had come to see Jesse as her father. It wasn't easy for any of us to accept, but those girls didn't want to be here. Tessa had a hard time with it too. She's never been the same since, losing her babies."

Ren could believe this answer. It made sense. Perhaps the girls' leaving was too painful for either Tal or Tessa to talk about. That was why they had been so distant to her.

Ren's doubts about this case were shifting. She was starting to wonder if maybe the residents at Shadow Rock were telling her the truth. Cedar had never been there.

A breeze had picked up and was blowing a fresh lavender scent into the smoke house. "Our workday is about to begin," Maude said. "Would you like to join us for our morning prayer?"

Ren declined with thanks. She had more pressing issues on her mind.

• • •

When Ren pulled into the gravel driveway at the inn, it was quiet. The Honeysuckle van was parked at the guesthouse, but there were few signs of activity. Ren entered the house and was relived to see that the kitchen was empty. Fat Elvis wasn't awake yet.

Ren went to her room and locked the door. She was still feeling shaky and confused. How had she made an error in judgment like that? She had been confident that her gun might protect her, but had been caught unawares by Jonah Ray.

These were the things she knew for sure: Ren had found a Greyhound ticket stub between Seattle and San Francisco in Cedar's bedroom. Bridge had told her that Cedar had gone down that way to find out about where she was born. Cedar's name had never been released to the media.

Those were the facts. Ren had believed what Jonah told her because he had known her name. Could he have overheard her talking about Cedar to Sean? Was there some illegal information about the case on the internet that Ren was unaware of? The story was getting some national attention. Maybe Jonah was following the news or had looked it up when the detectives showed up.

Or maybe he was telling the truth.

She sat on the bed for a long time. She wanted to take a long, hot shower, but she couldn't shake the feeling of fear. She wasn't sure how much time had passed before she got up. She looked at herself in the mirror. There was a spot of blood in the white bandaging on her forehead. It brought to mind the Japanese flag.

Ren needed to talk to Sean. She would tell him everything that happened and see what he thought. She removed her gun from its holster and took it with her as she walked down the hall to his room. She tapped on the door and waited. Outside, she could hear the guesthouse door slam and a car start. In the distance there was a steady stream of morning traffic. It was the day after Christmas and people were getting back to their lives.

Ren knocked again. When there was no answer, she turned the door handle.

She stepped into the room. The bed was made up, ready for the next guest. It was the same quilt she had seen him under when she left.

There was no sign of his clothes, phone, or even the wrapped gift Jenny had left him.

Sean was gone.

• • •

Ren stood in the empty room, wondering if she had stepped into the wrong one by accident. After a moment, she reached into her pocket and hit the speed dial. The phone rang a few times; then Sean's voice mail picked up. She listened to it, feeling oddly detached from her surroundings. Even Sean's voice sounded tinny and distant.

She exited the room. She had her gun and her cell and the keys to the rental car, which were the only things she would need. Downstairs, she heard Fat Elvis rattling around the kitchen, hitting the blender and throwing some butter in a frying pan. There was an eave outside her bedroom window that was about a ten-foot drop to the ground. The safest way out of the inn was through the kitchen. She had a plan to do it.

Ren moved down the stairs quickly. She paused before she entered the kitchen. She could hear bacon sizzling and smell coffee percolating. She moved silently, as rapidly as she could without making a sound. Fat Elvis had his back turned to her. He was scrambling eggs, singing some song about the night they drove old Dixie down.

Ren moved out of the kitchen and onto the porch, fearing that he was behind her. He was a huge mountain of a man; surely she would sense him if he had followed her. She threw her head around. No one was there.

Ren ran across the front lawn to the rental car. As she got in, she heard someone shouting her name. She turned the key, hit the gas petal, and reversed out of the driveway. As she turned into the street, she saw Jonah standing in the driveway.

Her hands were shaking on the wheel, and she couldn't focus. She ran a few stop signs and drove in circles, one eye in the rear view at all times. She thought of driving to the police station but decided against it. She drove until she found a hospital and pulled into the parking lot.

A young woman was behind the admittance desk as she entered. Ren walked right past her, flashing her badge as she went. She walked down the corridor, raking her head left and right. There were a dozen rooms, all made up immaculately.

The nurse was calling after her. Soon a security guard was making his way down the hall. Ren pulled out her badge and flashed it again. They both stopped in place, frozen by her authority.

Ren looked in the last room. It was blank and empty, a mirror image of the others. Why was it hospitals went for such shocking whiteness? It was like looking at death.

Something about that final room, with its impeccably made bed, made Ren break down. She felt hot salty tears that she couldn't hold back. She stood at the end of the hallway, her back turned from view, and let the weight of the case hit her. Three people were dead, she was in danger, and there was no end in sight.

She was alone, all alone, and she didn't know what to do.

CHAPTER TWENTY-THREE

Ren sat on the metal slab, swinging her feet like a child. She shivered in her paper gown. All she needed was a lollipop to complete the image of a girl at the pediatrician. What she wanted most right now was a warm pair of socks and her duvet. She thought of all her stuff locked in the Arts and Crafts Room at the Honeysuckle Inn. She wouldn't be going back there any time soon.

The nurse had given Ren a small paper cup of pills. They were hitting her bloodstream now. She felt slightly giddy, like she was tipsy.

The doctor breezed in. He was short with honey-blond hair and bushy eyebrows. He had a blue oxford on underneath his white coat. His name was Lester Vogel. "I am seeing injuries consistent with an assault," he said, sliding an X-ray onto an illuminated panel. Ren looked at the image of a skull in front on her.

"No serious damage, but you see that?" He pointed his pen at the top of the skull. "There is a slight protrusion. You may have been hit from behind by a rock."

Ren had no clearer sense of what had happened. She was feeling better, though—stronger.

"What do you know about Alvaro and Jenny Ray?" Ren asked the doctor. The words garbled out of her mouth. She strained for composure.

"I went to high school with his mother," Dr. Vogel said. "Johanna Tuff was her name. She was a bit of a wild child. Raised eyebrows by dating Mexicans. Married one too. I don't think her family ever recovered from that."

Ren thought of her partner and how he might respond to that remark. Sean was always telling Ren about the racism she never witnessed because of the color of her skin.

"Johanna died a while back. I went to her funeral," Dr. Vogel said. "I think Alvaro straightened out his life after that."

Ren nodded her head. Apparently townspeople knew about Fat Elvis's record.

"I'm going to sign this report for you," Dr. Vogel said. "Is there anything else that I can do for you while I'm here?"

The previous night was no less clear in her mind, but Ren knew what she had to do. "I need to talk to the police right away," she said. "And I need you to check the local morgue for a body."

Dr. Vogel shut off the light on the illuminated panel. "OK, I can get an officer here immediately. And who are we looking for at the morgue?"

"My partner," Ren said. "His name is Sean Lukela."

• • •

Ren sat alone in Dr. Vogel's office. She was still in her paper gown. The nurse had told her to take her time, and she was doing just that. She wasn't sure how long she had been sitting there when she heard her cell phone ring. The noise seemed to be coming through a shallow tunnel. Ren shook her head. She wished she had taken one less of those pills.

She answered the phone.

"Ren, what the hell is going on? I just got a call from the morgue. Have you lost your mind?"

"Sean?" she asked, relieved to hear his voice.

"I'm at the hospital in Castro. The police were just here and arrested Jonah. His mother is freaking out."

Sean explained what had happened. The previous night he had spiked a fever. Jenny had driven him to the hospital in Castro, which was just across the city line from Eplin. The doctors were talking about transferring him to San Francisco when his conditioned improved. They wanted him to stay at least overnight, so Jenny had brought him his things.

"You think Jonah tried to assault you?" Sean asked, taking her story in.

"I don't know what happened. The doctor seems to think I was hit in the head. I should be free in a minute here. I'm going to come find you."

• • •

Ren emerged into the bright light of an Eplin morning. Her car was in the parking lot, zigzagging across two spots. It wasn't so much parked as abandoned. She had been in a state when she arrived there. She remembered her frenzied mind, her lack of focus. She was much calmer now.

Ren got into the car and entered Castro General Hospital into the GPS. Soon the GPS lady was directing her in her flat hall monitor voice. Ren took a right out of the hospital parking lot onto the main thoroughfare. She passed a library, a courthouse, and a historical society. Beyond that was a commercial district with gift shops, a cafe, and a '50s-style drive-thru. After a stoplight, the street gave way to a residential neighborhood.

The city limit was after an elementary school. The school was closed for the holidays, the flagpole bare and the schoolyard deserted. As she entered Castro, Ren spotted the Taj Mahal. It was hard to miss: there was a replica of the white palace on a rotating pole. Ren would visit there later to see if she could talk to the woman in the turquoise sari. It was a safe bet that a white woman dressed in a sari might know something about the town's religious subculture. What Ren needed most right now was an objective witness. Those were proving a little hard to come by.

But first Ren had to see her partner. She couldn't wait to see him again.

• • •

When Ren entered Castro General Hospital through the sliding glass doors, the last thing she was expecting to see was someone's fist. And yet that is what greeted her, a collection of knuckles hurtling at her at tremendous speed. She saw the fingers, and the gold rings on each them, and felt the impact of the blow.

"You think my baby is some kind of rapist?" Jenny screamed from the floor. A security guard had tackled her from behind, and she was now flailing there on top of him, trying to break free of him with the force of her strength. She looked like a bug that had fallen on its back.

Ren stood on the entrance mat, holding her face in her hands. The glass doors were opening and shutting behind her like windshield wipers. She stepped off the mat to make them stop.

Ren walked to the nurses' station, still holding her nose. The woman behind the desk handed her some towels. Ren wiped her face and held a towel firm against her nose to slow the bleeding. This was the second time she'd had seen blood today, and she was getting tired of it. On her wrist she was still wearing the chunky bracelet Jenny had given her for Christmas.

"Would you like to press charges?" the security guard asked.

"Yes," Ren said. "Throw her in a cell with her son."

Ren moved back into the corridor. She didn't need directions. In the last few hours she had become intimately familiar with the layout of small-town hospitals. She found Sean sitting up in bed in the last room to the left.

"Yikes," he said, putting down his spoon. His mouth was full of cubes of cherry Jell-O. "He did that to you?"

Ren looked at herself in the wall mirror. She looked like she had just emerged from plastic surgery. At least the nurse at the hospital in Eplin had removed the Japanese flag from her forehead. She was covered in clean, white gauze now, something like a bird's nest on her head.

"It was a mother/son act," she said. "Apparently Jenny's not too thrilled about what happened up at the rocks." She took a seat next to the bed. Her pulse was throbbing in her ear. On the wall a TV played *Miracle on 34th Street*. "How are you feeling, anyway?"

"The IV drip helped," Sean said. "I should be getting out of here soon. Not a bad place to spend Christmas. Turns out Castro is where they stash all the brown people. Did you see that nurse? I'm calling her my J. Lo."

"Did you get the message from Henry Wu?" he asked her.

Ren shook her head, then looked at her phone. There was one message she hadn't picked up. She must have lost service for a few moments driving over.

"They've pulled up some content from Ruby's website. Looks like she was amateur sleuthing and thought she had found the killer. You can see the document right there on my laptop."

He motioned to a table next to the bed. Ren walked over and opened his email. There was a message from Henry with an attachment. It was a reconstruction of content from Ruby's site. Ren opened the file and read it:

A Tale of Two Girls

Tongues have been wagging for months now. How did a young woman, a runaway, end up dead in the house of Lydia Merton? Is Lydia really as innocent as she claims? Police have their theories; journalists have their theories. So far they're both wrong.

I am about to take you on a journey. You will be a different person when this four-part series is over. You will wonder how it is police have messed this up. You will know why an innocent girl died.

The problem, dear reader, is that the detectives never found me.

Ren finished reading and shut the laptop.

"So Ruby had information that might have helped us, but she held back in the name of sensationalism?"

"I don't know about that, Ren. She may have just been blowing smoke, trying to create controversy."

Ren was feeling slightly irked for missing this information when it came through. Sean must have gotten the email from Henry while she was knocked out by the rocks. "So whoever killed Ruby must have seen the website content. Her sleuthing got her killed."

"Henry said there were over two hundred hits by the time the site was disabled. It's a needle in a haystack all over again."

Ren ignored him and checked her phone. He was doing a lot of complaining for someone who hadn't lifted a finger since they'd gotten to California.

There was nothing in her inbox from Henry Wu. He must

have forgotten to email her. But someone had left Ren a voice message from a local area code. She dialed in and listened to it. Then she got up.

"Where are you going?" Sean asked. "You just got here."

"I've got an errand to do. If I'm not back in thirty minutes, call me."

Ren exited the room and walked down the hallway. She did have an errand to do, but before she did it, she had decided to answer the voice message in person. She was going to talk to Jonah Ray.

• • •

The bailiff was a squat Latina woman with blue eye shadow and peacock feathers hanging from hoops in her ears. Apparently there wasn't much of a dress code at the Castro County Jail. There wasn't much of an interior either: Ren could see the holding area from reception. There were two cells, apparently segregated by gender. Jenny and Jonah occupied one each.

"You here to apologize to us, or to let us out?" Jenny asked. She had her legs crossed and was reading a *PEOPLE* magazine.

"Neither," Ren said. She walked over to Jonah's cell and stood squarely in front of it. He had used his one call to leave her a message. She had given him her cell number the first encounter she had with him, when he had ID'd Cedar from the police sketch. That seemed like a long time ago now.

She had listened to his message a second time on the way over: *I didn't assault you, Ms. Copeland. I swear to you. Someone attacked us. Give me a chance to explain.*

"Jonah," Ren said. "You've got five minutes to tell me what happened up there."

• • •

Ren drove the main drag in Castro. On the radio, a raspy-voiced woman with frizzy hair and a lacy shawl was singing about the landslide bringing it down. Ren wasn't listening. Instead she was thinking of what Jonah had just told her.

"*After I tried to kiss you, you walked away. I watched you as you went. I stepped behind the rocks and out of nowhere, someone grabbed me from behind. All I could feel was my hair being pulled. Then I blacked out. When I came to, I was halfway down the incline. It was pitch black. I thought I was alone out there so I walked to the village, but everyone was asleep. I walked back to town. I got home at about 3 a.m. My parents were asleep, and I went to bed. The next morning I saw you leaving the inn, and I called out to you, but you had driven way by the time I got near you.*"

Ren wasn't sure what to think of Jonah's story. It was possible he was telling the truth. He had pointed to some wounds on his face from a fall. Someone may have attacked him behind the rocks and then done the same to her. Perhaps she had misjudged him. He was young, after all. It was possible he had tried to kiss her without any sinister intent and what happened later was unrelated to it.

But that left the question of who had assaulted them. Ren knew of five adult residents at Shadow Rock: Tal, Maude, Tessa West, and the geisha girls. It was possible one of them had seen Jonah and Ren at the rocks and snuck up on them. But what had motivated them?

Ren turned off into a driveway. Towering over her was a replica of the Taj Mahal, moving slowly in rotation on a pole. There was a neon sign beneath it that read *six types of chutney*.

Ren walked to the entrance. It was closed so she peered through the Plexiglas. A man in a turban and golden robes was going over some receipts. He didn't look up.

Ren was about to leave when she saw a woman getting off

a city bus, a straw bag thrown over her shoulder. The bus was tiny, like the kind that transports preschoolers. The woman was dressed in flaming red. Ren imagined she had a closet with one sari in every color.

"I'm a little late today," she said to Ren as she approached. "I figured, who wants vindaloo on Boxing Day?" She spoke with a muted British accent.

"I was hoping I might talk to you," Ren said. "Can you spare an extra minute before you go in?"

The woman's face flushed. "I suppose so. I am the owner."

Ren was taken aback. The 76 clerk had said she was a waitress. And how many business owners ride the city bus?

"I saw you walking yesterday in Eplin," Ren said.

"We're a one-car family," the woman said. "I sometimes walk to work or take the bus."

She looked at Ren a bit more intently. "You look like you've had better days."

Ren touched her forehead. She was almost forgetting about the bandages wrapped around her. She glanced at her reflection. She looked like a mummy.

The woman removed a heavy set of keys from her bag and opened the front door. She motioned for Ren to follow her in. The interior was painted black, and the walls were covered with velvet paintings depicting various images from *The Bhagavad-Gita*. The man in the golden robes walked over. They kissed.

"This is my husband, Ravi," the woman said. "And you are?"

Ren introduced herself.

"I'm Janice Dixon," the woman said, taking a seat opposite Ren at a table. Then she shouted over her shoulder, "Ravi, can you get us some ice water?" She fanned herself with a menu.

"How long has the place been open?" Ren asked.

Janice eyed Ren's badge, which she had laid on the table. "Ten years now. Chicken tikka masala is the favored dish. Keeps us in the black."

"You're not from the area, I take it?"

"No, I'm from Oxford. I'm half-British. Went to India when I was a student, met Ravi, and we ended up in San Francisco. Moved out here when we wanted a yard for the kids. Less competition as well. We get people from five towns in the area driving here for our buffet."

Ravi appeared with glasses of ice water and a pot of tea. He set them down next to Ren's badge.

"I'm wondering if you know anything about Shadow Rock," Ren asked. She pulled out the sketch of Cedar.

"Certainly," Janice said. "I've driven by a few times. Some people mock the place, but I am impressed by the austerity." She looked at the sketch and then dug into her bag for a pair of eyeglasses. After considering the image for a moment, she shook her head.

Ren took the sketch back. So far Jonah was the only one who had ID'd Cedar from it.

"I'm not religious myself," Janice said. "I was in Varanasi once and saw a woman throw herself on her husband's funeral pyre. All I could think was, maybe this woman understands something about faith that I can't grasp. But Ravi told me I was being too romantic. The truth was that her only alternative was a life of misery."

Ren took a sip of water. "You don't know any of the residents at Shadow Rock?"

Janice shook her head. "They don't come into town much. My daughter told me some story that she heard at a sleepover. There are rumors that a woman was murdered out there twenty years ago and that her ghost still haunts the land."

"You think there is any truth to that? About the murder, I mean."

"My first thought was that it sounded a lot like a story I heard about the Yorkshire ripper when I was growing up. Some horror stories are universal. They seem to get told a lot at sleepovers."

Ren nodded. She was going to look up the story to see if there was anything to it. "Do you know of any place in town I could get internet access today? The library or something?"

"It's not open today. They take a break along with the schools," Janice said. "But we've got a computer in my office that you could use."

Ren followed Janice back to a dingy office just off the kitchen. She could smell spices and fresh bread in the hallway as they walked. When the aroma hit her, she realized just how hungry she was. The last thing she'd had to eat was that peanut butter cookie from the 76 station.

"Is there any way I could trouble you for a plate of food?" Ren asked. "I'll pay of course."

Janice powered up the computer and motioned to Ren to take the seat in front of it. Then she scurried out and returned with a heaping plate of lamb masala, rice, and naan. Ren ate it rapaciously.

After thirty minutes, Ren had found a few articles. The local press had documented the mysterious vanishing of a young woman and her eventual memorial service. There was a photo of Tal and Maude at the service, sitting next to an elderly couple that Ren assumed were the girl's parents.

She was twenty when she disappeared in 1994, a native of Eplin. Her name was Dixie Larkin.

Her parents were listed as Vernon and Clare Larkin. She also had a sister named Daisy. Ren ran the names through the white pages. There was a D. Larkin listed in Eplin. Ren scribbled down the address and phone number.

As she left, Ren grabbed a few triangles of naan for the road.

"Find what you're looking for?" Janice asked as Ren exited the hallway. She was filling glass jars with a red spice. Ravi was placing napkins at tables.

"We'll see," Ren said.

• • •

When Ren reached the address on Wilson Street, she turned off into the driveway. In front of her as she parked were two motorcycles. The belly of one was streaked with images of flames. The other had a leather-fringed seat. The house was white clapboard with a sunken front porch.

Ren walked up onto the porch and knocked. After a moment a burly blonde woman answered the door. She was nearly three hundred pounds and towered over Ren by nearly six inches. She was wearing jeans and a blue work shirt. There was a label above her heart with a name stitched on it. *Daisy*.

Daisy winked at her. "Are you my Christmas gift?" she asked.

Ren flashed her badge and asked if she could come in. There was an evergreen tree in the front window dripping with silver tinsel and red glitter balls. A pair of Chihuauas yapped around their feet as they walked back into the living room.

Daisy leaned down and pulled a dog into each hand. "This is Mitzi and Maisie. They are madly in love with each other."

The dogs looked at Ren with beady, eager eyes. They were probably wishing they could lick her bloody wounds.

"I know better than to ask who did that to you," Daisy said, sinking into a recliner the color of pea soup. The dogs settled into her lap. "I've been there. Any time I'm late with shop payments, I'm running scared."

Ren had never traded war stories of this kind. She feared she'd sound like a rank amateur if she tried.

"I understand you have ties to Shadow Rock."

"Not exactly," Daisy said. "My sister lived out there many years ago."

Ren nodded. "Your sister?"

"Yes, Dixie. She died about seventeen years ago."

"Oh, I'm sorry," Ren said. "How did she die?"

"The police have never solved it. The residents at Shadow Rock reported her missing one summer. I was in the service at the time and was living in Okinawa. Got a call that they found Dixie's suitcase in a locker at a bus station but no trace of her. After a certain number of years, they had her declared dead, just to give my parents that peace before they died."

"You were in the military at the time she lived at Shadow Rock?"

"Yup," Daisy said. "I applied for a leave when my sister was declared dead. I had to come home to help my parents deal with that."

"What do you think happened?" Ren asked her.

Daisy looked off in the distance, as if remembering something. "My sister is dead. I can feel it in my bones. Something happened to her, and her body has never been found. I'm not convinced those freaks out there don't know something about it. But now that my parents are gone, I just don't have it in me to look for her anymore. I have learned that some mysteries just don't get solved."

"I'm so sorry," Ren said. She thought of the lonely holiday Daisy must have just had. It was the hardest part of her job, meeting people like this.

"May I see a photo of your sister?" Ren asked. She had seen a high school portrait of Dixie in the news stories. She was fair and plain, which seemed to be true of most of the women at Shadow Rock. She would have fit right in.

Daisy set the dogs on the floor and heaved herself up from her chair. She went into a back room. She was gone a while. When she came back she was holding a framed photo. It was one of those professional portraits that make everyone look like taxidermy. It was the two sisters as teenagers. Daisy was on the left, plump and happy. Dixie was next to her, willowy and freckled.

It was hard to say for sure, but Dixie and Cedar might have been mother and daughter. It was possible.

"Daisy, what happened to your sister's children after she died?" Ren asked.

Daisy took a seat again. Mitzi and Maisie scampered around her feet.

"Children?" she asked. "My sister didn't have any. I am the end of the family line."

• • •

"So we've got a young woman who looks a bit like Cedar who disappeared seventeen years ago. And her dyke sister doesn't know she had any kids. And we've got Jonah with some memory of being at Shadow Rock. He thinks he was born there too."

Sean was puzzling over what Ren had just told him. She was half-listening as she looked at a file of news clippings Daisy had given her. It was the same articles she had found on Janice's computer, but this would save her having to get online again.

"You think they killed her? Buried her body at Shadow Rock and made it look like she fled?"

Ren shook her head. "I don't know."

"Maybe they were harvesting kids out there, like organs? Tricking young women into getting pregnant and then giving their kids up for adoption? There could be money in that."

Ren kicked her feet up onto Sean's hospital bed. The TV on the wall was now playing *It's a Wonderful Life*.

"So, what are we going to do?" Sean asked her. "Go through another round of interviews where everyone denies knowing anything?"

Ren slumped back in her chair. It was just starting to hit her how exhausted she was.

After a moment she said, "I think we have one last option."

• • •

The woman with the peacock feathers was still on duty when Ren showed up. A stocky man dressed in denim with a white beard was there as well. He removed his cowboy hat and introduced himself as Hank Franklin, the Ray family attorney.

Jenny Ray was where Ren had left her. She had moved on to a paperback novel, an Australian saga about a priest and his doomed love affair. She was engrossed in it as Ren approached the cell. She didn't look up until her lawyer addressed her.

Jenny's arraignment was scheduled for later that day, but it was looking now like that wasn't going to happen. The three of them moved from the holding area into an interview room.

"I'm prepared to make you a deal," Ren told her after they sat down. "I will drop the assault charges if you give me something I can work with. I can offer you immunity if you've done something illegal."

She didn't relish letting her off with a slap on the wrist, but this was her best chance to get something on record. Without it, the trip had been for naught. Ren was betting the house on her hunch that Jenny didn't have anything to do with Cedar's murder. This was quite a claim, given that the woman had assaulted her earlier that day.

Jenny cocked her head to the side. She and Hank Franklin huddled for a few moments in consultation. She said something to him, and he nodded. Then Jenny turned and stared at Ren. Her eyes were cold.

"Jonah is not my son," Jenny said. "His name is not even Jonah. He was born at Shadow Rock."

CHAPTER TWENTY-FOUR

Ren awoke to the sound of a braying Wookiee. She was wrapped in blankets on her couch, bone tired, but the sunlight and the insistent bleating roused her. She could tell that it was early. She sat up.

Ariel, Ren's marmalade kitty, brayed away near her water dish. She had earned the nickname Chewbacca due to her raucous meowing, which made her sound more like a Wookiee than a housecat. This was especially true in the early morning, when Ariel wanted fresh water and to get outside.

"I hope you will be well enough for the party tomorrow night," Ramon said, emerging from the bathroom. He was dressed in his clothes from yesterday. "Lie back down. I'll deal with Chewie. We're still not letting you move today."

Ren did as she was told, returning to the couch. She looked up into the loft and saw that her mother was stirring. Ramon and Bebe had stayed the night.

In front of her on the coffee table, the granite faces of Abe Lincoln and Teddy Roosevelt stared back at her. They had worked on a puzzle of Mount Rushmore for several hours last night, after watching a Doris Day movie. Bebe had made lemongrass soup.

It was four days later, and Ren was back in Seattle. She had left Eplin with more than she'd gone there with: she had a statement from Jenny Ray in exchange for an immunity deal. Ren refused to negotiate Jonah's assault charges. The more time she had time to think about it, the less she believed his story. The most logical explanation for what had happened at the rocks was the one she was going with. He would have to face the consequences of his actions.

"I can't believe Sean left you alone like that," Bebe said as she walked down the loft stairs in one of Ren's silk kimonos. Puck was resting on her shoulder. He opened his wingspan for a stretch, revealing an iridescent blue.

Ren ignored her mother's comment. The truth was, Ren blamed herself for what happened. She had believed Jonah because she trusted him, and also because she wanted to crack the case. It had cost her this time. She was looking forward to going back to work and proving to herself that she could settle this without taking unnecessary risks.

"Do you feel up to waffles this morning?" Ramon asked from the kitchen. He was about to grind some coffee beans.

"I don't have a waffle iron," Ren said. It was true: too much temptation.

"Pancakes, then?"

What Ren really wanted to do was to go for a long run. She hadn't had time for one while she was in Eplin. This was the longest she had gone without endorphins in some time. She missed them. "I'm going to be fine with just coffee and oatmeal. You two go ahead."

Ren's cell phone rang as Ramon was washing up. Bebe was upstairs making the bed. Puck was with her, squawking for attention. Ariel had been let loose to prowl the docks. "What's the word?"

"I've got good news and bad."

"Worst first."

"The judge in Eplin has ruled that the doctor's examination is inadmissible. Looks like it's your word against his."

"Great, he'll get off with a slap on the wrist. Justice is served."

Ren still wasn't sure what had happened to her up at the rocks, but she could come up with no other plausible explanation for what had happened. Most likely Jonah had lashed out at her for rejecting him and then felt remorse the next day and come up with a cover story. He had been telling the truth about his interactions with Cedar, but his motives for going with Ren to the rocks were suspect.

"Also I ran the license plates. Nothing is turning up."

Sean was talking about the plates for Tal's truck and the Honeysuckle van. Ren had taken them down to see if either vehicle had been spotted in Seattle. "I've got better news too. Remember when I told you that Lieutenant Roemer ordered Bridge Heekin's phone records?"

She did. He had told her that on Christmas. It seemed so long ago now. "Yes, what have you found?"

"I've been looking over them, and there are four calls between his number and Jesse West's number."

"Cedar's stepfather and Ruby's father had contact?"

"Yes, in July. I talked to Bridge, and he swears that it was Cedar making those calls. He said that she had come back to the house to pick up some stuff. It was the last time he saw her."

"You believe him?"

"I think so. Bridge doesn't seem to talk to anyone. There is almost no activity on his phone other than food delivery. I think he's just a lonely, depressed guy. Anyway, we're bringing Jesse West in for questioning. Roemer has offered him immunity in exchange for what he knows. I think we'll get something for that."

"I am going to need to be there for that. What he says will give me a better idea whether I can believe what Jenny Ray told me."

Ren flashed on an image of Ruby's mother in the smoke house at Shadow Rock, the way she had swatted her hand through the air and disappeared without saying a word. She was curious to meet the man who was once married to her.

"He's coming in tomorrow," Sean said as he rang off. "I'll see you then."

Ren picked up the birth certificate that sat on her coffee table. It was for a boy named Mulberry Bush Rasmussen, born May 3, 1993 in Eplin. If what Jenny had told her was true, this certificate could blow open the case.

They were about to meet the man who could confirm or deny it.

• • •

It had been a few days, and Lydia finally had the foghorn out of her head. She could feel the waves beneath her still, the choppy water under the car as they moved toward some unseen destination. They had been on a boat, she knew that much, most likely a ferry leading somewhere. She could have been anywhere.

Lydia came to in the trunk of a car. She didn't remember getting there. She could see the trail at Interlaken in her mind's eye and feel the soft earth beneath her feet. She remembered seeing the figure coming at her. That was all.

Lydia's hair was matted with dried blood, and her arms throbbed in the quilted jacket. It was bound tight like swaddling clothes. Her hands and feet were tied. Her mouth was covered with duct tape. It was ripping at the hairs on her face. She had never felt such pain.

Lydia had read somewhere that the best way to escape being locked in a car trunk was to smash out the taillight from inside. Alas, her attacker seemed to have access to the same information and had bound Lydia so tightly there was no way she could do any damage. For the duration of the ferry ride

Lydia's brain was in overdrive, but with only one thing on her mind: she had to escape.

She had felt the car inch forward and then roll more freely as it reached land. They drove for several miles before turning off onto a gravel road. They traveled farther before the car came to a full stop. Lydia was gasping from exhaust fumes. Her kidnapper moved around a bit, opening a garage door and then closing it.

Lydia must have blacked out again, because when she came to she was in a pitch-black room. It was dank and smelled of mold. There was empty space around her, which felt liberating after being in the trunk so long. She still had the swaddling on her, but a device had been added. It was some kind of GPS tracker.

Lydia had been here now for days. She had some water but no food. The foghorn had stopped but she could still feel the boat under her. She remembered what her kidnapper had said it to her when they reached land. It stuck in her mind like a clarion call. She wished she could stop the repetitive loop of the words, over and over and over, but she heard it constantly: *I'm going to kill you. But first I'm going to figure out who you are.*

CHAPTER TWENTY-FIVE

Jesse West had had one blessing in life, and if he had been a believer, he would have thanked God every day for it. When he lived at Shadow Rock, he had seen evil. There were many people who had been spared this experience, and they thought they were the lucky ones. Jesse knew better. He was the lucky one.

Until he had experienced evil, Jesse thought of it as some nebulous force that takes possession of people, like a spirit in a horror movie. He didn't know that evil is not a force but rather a void. And once he saw that void he worked every day of his life to never step into it. His love for his daughters kept him from falling.

His memories of Shadow Rock were buried in the past when the Seattle PD came calling. The last thing he wanted to do was to unearth that time in his life again. It was a lesson to him: sometimes you have no choice but to face things.

He met the detectives at the Seattle East precinct. Talia came with him. She took a seat in the lobby, accepting the offer of a Coke and a Hostess cherry pie. The last thing he remembered as he entered the interview room was looking back at her sweet face.

"I never met Cedar Heekin," Jesse told them after he'd settled in. He could see his reflection in the mirror on the wall opposite him. It gave off a slightly warped image. "But she started calling my house last summer. She said she had found my name in some writings by Lydia Merton."

"Why don't we start at the beginning," Ren said. "Tell us how you came to live at Shadow Rock."

Jesse told them the story. It hadn't been his idea to move there. He had a wife and baby, and he worked as an artisan, traveling up and down the California coast. One winter, they were so broke that they'd accepted the generosity of Tal Rasmussen. It was meant to be temporary. Jesse could spot right away that Shadow Rock was Tal's kingdom. He had no intention of being a serf. When he was back on his feet again, he had moved away and never returned. His daughters had gone with him.

"What else did Cedar say to you when you talked to her?" Sean asked.

"She believed that she had been lied to about how she made it into the world. She was trying to get some answers."

"And could you help her? Did you have information for her?"

Jesse hung his head. He was remembering that day many years ago when the woman stepped into the void and abandoned her babies. "I had the information she needed," he said. "But I didn't give it to her. I told her I didn't know anything. I think that is why my daughter is dead." Jesse began to cry. The full weight of the last few months was hitting him.

"You're going to need to tell us what you know, Jesse," Ren said. "We have to stop these killings."

He seemed visibly relieved as he began talking. "Cedar's mother was a woman named Dixie. She was from town. She was eighteen when she moved out there. She had a son with Tal and then a year later, a daughter with him as well. She couldn't handle the life there, so she took off. We never saw her again."

Ren was thinking of her day at the rocks with Jonah. Dixie could have been the woman he remembered. He had told her the truth. His memory was real. "Why didn't you tell Cedar her mother was named Dixie? Give her that clarity?"

"Because we forged a birth certificate," Jesse said. "We could have gone to jail." He paused. "There is more."

They waited.

"Cedar told me that she thought she had found her biological mother. She thought it was a woman named Lydia Merton."

Here it was: the final piece of the puzzle. Cedar had targeted that house for a particular reason: she thought it belonged to her mother.

"Lydia can't be Cedar's mother," Sean said. "The dates don't make sense. She would have been what, sixteen, when Cedar was born? Plus she told us she never participated in the ceremonies. She was just a guest."

"I think someone gave her Lydia's name when Cedar visited Shadow Rock," Jesse said. "Maybe they thought it would throw her off the scent."

"So someone lied to her and told her her mother was named Lydia Merton."

Jesse nodded. "I know who Cedar's real mother was," he said. "I helped her give birth. Her name was Dixie Larkin."

The three of them sat in silence for a moment. Ren could tell that Jesse had more to say.

"I remember seeing Dixie a few days after she gave birth to Cedar. She just wasn't there anymore. I don't think she even suckled that baby once. There was this void she stepped into after she had the second one. I saw Tessa go into it too, after Talia was born. Tal Rasmussen's vision of life and motherhood was just wrong. The kids have really suffered for it." He had expressed similar criticisms of Shadow Rock to those in Lydia's thesis.

"I was overwhelmed trying to take care of those kids. Ruby and Talia were small. Tessa was checked out herself. She wasn't as bad as Dixie, but she wasn't fully engaged either."

Ren was starting to understand it all now. The strange way Tessa had behaved the day they met was less about grief and more about her damaged mental state. It explained why the girls had left with Jesse and had little relationship with their mother since that time.

"Cedar and Mully needed a mother. There was no one to step in to fill the absence when Dixie left. After about five months, we just couldn't handle it anymore. Tal knew some people who wanted to adopt but couldn't do it legally. So we arranged for them to take the kids. It was against the law, but Tal believed he had found the right people to raise his kids."

Ren had one birth certificate in front of her. Mulberry Bush was born in May 1993.

"Mulberry Rasmussen became Jonah Ray," Ren said. She pulled out another birth certificate, this one for Jonah. It had the same birth date, but listed his parents as Alvaro Ray and Jenny Fitch. "This is a fraudulent certificate. They are not his biological parents. They couldn't adopt a child legally because of Fat Elvis's record."

"Tal knew someone who worked the black market. He arranged to get those fake certificates. The kids never knew they had been adopted."

"So Dixie and Tal's son ended up with the Rays. What about Cedar?"

"She was adopted by a woman that Tal met at one of the artisan fairs," Jesse said. "She had this whole sob story about how all she wanted was a baby, but that she couldn't adopt because she had had leukemia as a girl. Tal felt that this woman was meant to be the girl's mother, so he arranged for her to take her. Same situation as Jonah, but it was to a single mother who moved to Washington."

This was making sense. A woman abandoned her kids, and Tal saw it as his providential duty to find them families, even if they broke the law to do it. All of this was consistent with what Ren knew of Tal. What he didn't count on was the kids growing up and looking into it.

"Jesse, do you have any idea what happened to Dixie Larkin? Is it possible some harm came to her?" Ren was thinking of what Daisy Larkin had told her, about her gut instinct that her sister was dead.

Jesse shook his head. "No harm came to her that I know of. She told me before she left that her family was abusive and she couldn't go back to them. She had a plan to get away for good. When I asked her what she was going to do, she said she was going to take the name of another resident that had lived at Shadow Rock for a time. She thought she could run away and make a new life for herself."

"So Dixie abandoned her kids and stole someone's identity when she left," Ren said. "Do you remember the name she took?"

Ren and Sean were not at all prepared for what they heard next.

"Betty," Jesse said. "Dixie took the name of a resident named Betty Holland."

•   •   •

When Jesse West's interview wrapped up, Ren and Sean were gorged with details. They sat back at the interview room table, fat like slugs.

Their first order of business was to get a DNA sample from Sister Betty Holland at the Westside Home for Girls. If she refused, they would get a warrant.

"You think the nun is the mother of Cedar and Jonah?" Sean asked. "What are the odds these details are unconnected?"

"I don't know; it's not an uncommon name," Ren said. "Let's proceed with caution."

Ren and Sean walked back to their desks. Ren got on the phone to the sheriff in Eplin. She needed DNA samples from Jonah Ray and Jenny Ray. She was reasonably certain she could get them without a court order; Jenny's assault charges had been dropped due to a deal Ren had offered her. She had agreed to testify with immunity about Jonah's biological parents if it ever came to trial. Sean got on the phone to the Westside Home for Girls.

Ren was mid-sentence with the Eplin sheriff when she felt an insistent tap on her shoulder. This was unusual: she hadn't been approached this way since the nuns at Veronica Prep. She turned around, giving the international symbol for "one minute" to her interrupter. Behind her, Joshua Conlin gave the international symbol for "get off the phone, pronto." Someone passing by might have thought they were mimes.

Ren was in no mood for Conlin's pettiness. She ignored him until she wrapped up her call. She glanced over at Sean. He gave her a shake of the head: he was evidently getting nowhere with Sister Betty.

After she hung up, Ren turned around. "Can I help you with something, Joshua?"

"Detective Copeland, I need to talk to you privately," he said. He always spoke in formal honorifics, showing a respect to the ranks that he never showed to the people who held them. Ren wasn't fooled by it; it was Conlin's way of honoring the badge without honoring its people.

"We're in the middle of something here. Can it wait?" Ren asked. They had just spent five hours taking Jesse West's statement.

"I think you're going to want to hear what I have to say, and I think you're going to want to hear it in private." He turned on his heel and walked back toward the empty interview room.

Ren got up and followed him, shrugging at Sid and Jason as she passed their desks. She stepped back into the interview room. She'd been seeing a lot of it recently.

"Detective Copeland, I've been processing the crime scene to a burglary that happened recently," Conlin said to her. "Homeowner came back from a trip only to find that his property had been tampered with. He filed a report."

Ren nodded. It was sounding a bit like the Merton house. She wondered if he'd found something, a parallel crime.

"We isolated one set of prints that don't belong to a family member," Conlin said. "Imagine my surprise when I ran them through the database and found they were a match."

This was big news. Ren focused her attention on Conlin, showing him respect for the first time in their interaction. Maybe she had misjudged him. She'd been doing that a lot lately.

"Whose prints are they?" Ren asked.

"They're yours," Conlin said.

CHAPTER TWENTY-SIX

"The break-in was at 1409 Aloha," Ren said to Conlin. It was more of a statement than a question. "The Hutching residence."

"Yes, detective. I don't even want to know how you knew that so quickly."

Milton was back in Seattle, apparently. He had discovered that Delphine had skipped town, so he'd filed a police report on the property, claiming a burglary. That meant Del's prints were now updated in the system. All he would have to do is name her as the likely suspect, and she would get stopped at borders. A routine traffic stop could get her pulled in. An arrest warrant against Delphine was the closest thing Milton had to a GPS tracker.

God, he was good.

Ren knew what was coming next. The detectives assigned to the case would contact Milton with the news about the prints they had discovered. Milton would tell them that his meth addict daughter had broken into the property when he was out of town. There would be a warrant issued. If Delphine had gotten to Anchorage already and could stay out of trouble, she might have a shot at outsmarting her father.

Ren pushed the images out of her mind. She could not be involved. She had a case to solve.

"My only explanation for my prints being there is that I have been in that house many times. I went to high school with Delphine Hutching."

"You're telling me these prints are from years ago?"

"I have no idea when they're from," Ren lied. "But I suspect if you tell Milton that they belong to me, he won't blink. He's not going to believe I was behind this. Our families go way back to Veronica Prep."

Ren rarely name dropped, but her education was a passport that could get her out of moments like this. Men like Conlin were lapdogs to the rich and powerful. Ren knew that this kind of detail would detract him.

"I have to report back what I found to the detectives assigned to this," Conlin said. "I can't break the chain of command."

Ren stared at him blankly. He was testing her, to see if she'd ask him to suppress his findings. What Sean had told her on Christmas was right; it was only a matter of time until Conlin was fully in control. He was just that focused on it.

"You do what you need to do," Ren said. "I've got a case to close, Joshua. Are the West/Rasmussen DNA samples on their way to the lab?"

"We put a rush order on them. Two days tops."

Ren thanked him and left the room.

• • •

It was early January, but signs of the holidays remained. Nola had not removed the sleigh bell attached to the front door on the third floor, which rang cheerfully as people came and went. Snow was still spray-painted on windows, creating a wistful winter feeling. It gave Ren and Sean the feeling of doing their job in Santa's workshop.

"There is one thing I don't understand," Sean said. He was looking at the case file while Ren highlighted some phone records. "Why did Cedar think that Lydia was her mother? Couldn't she tell from reading the thesis that the timeline was off?"

Ren got up from her desk to stretch. She was almost ready

for her afternoon snack and was deciding between granola bars and pretzels. "I don't know how closely Cedar read the thesis," she said. "I didn't see any sign of a computer at Bridge's house, and she was homeless on and off. She may have just viewed that website from a ten-minute terminal at the library or something."

Sid Hopkins loped over from the other side of the room to join them. He was carrying a thick manila envelope, which he dropped on Sean's desk. "Nola spilled the beans about Pablo," he said. "You won, Hula boy."

Sean pulled out a stack of crisp twenties. Ren shot him a look of disapproval.

"Don't you even want to know how I figured it out?" he asked her. "This was keen detective work on my part."

Ren said nothing.

The sleigh bell rang merrily as Nola entered with a padded envelope and a small cardboard box. Sean and Ren looked at her expectantly.

"Sorry," she said, and dropped the items on Jason's desk.

Ren and Sean were waiting patiently for the DNA results. They were due back from the lab any moment now.

They had Jesse West's statement about the year a woman named Betty Holland showed up at Shadow Rock. Dixie had stolen her identity when she ran away from her life. The results would confirm whether Sister Betty Holland had anything to do with these events. They had gotten a warrant for her DNA after she had refused an interview.

The sleigh bell rang again. A man in a purple FedEx uniform strode in the room. He walked over to Ren's desk. She jumped up, excited, and signed for it. Ren tore open the package. Sean walked over and read over Ren's shoulder. There was a whole stack of papers to look through, results from the DNA lab.

Here is what they said:

Sister Betty Holland was biologically related to Cedar, the victim. She was also biologically related to Jonah Ray. She was also biologically related to Daisy Larkin, who had offered a sample when Ren called her to tell her what she'd found.

The results left them with little doubt. Sister Betty Holland was Dixie Larkin.

"Wow," Sean said, sinking back into his swivel chair. "Do you think our nun killed her kid?"

"I don't know," Ren said. "All I know is we have enough for a warrant to bring her in." She would also call in a request for phone and computer records at the Westside Home for Girls, to see if there was any evidence of contact between Cedar and Sister Betty. And as soon as she was done with that, she would call Daisy Larkin and let her know that her sister was alive. Calls like that were among the strangest things Ren had to do on the job. She had done it a handful of times working missing persons cases.

But first, they would find out what Sister Betty Holland had to say for herself.

• • •

Sister Betty Holland brought a lawyer with her, a pit bull of a guy with a short, clipped beard and thin lips named Leo Bassan. Ren had encountered him before when he worked for the public defender's office. They met in an interview room: Betty and Leo on one side, Ren and Sean on the other.

"What do you have to say for yourself?" Sean asked. He was quite shocked by her deception.

"I moved to the village when I was eighteen. I was quite taken with it, for a time. But when Mully was born, my life took a turn."

"Mully?" Sean said. "Don't you know he goes by the name Jonah now?"

Sister Betty ignored the comment. "What do you want me to tell you? Tal and I had two babies in two years, and when I couldn't take it anymore, I left them with their father. They were in good hands."

Sean snorted. "Weren't you at all concerned about them? You had to get out, but your kids could stay?"

"Shadow Rock is a harmless place," Sister Betty said. "I was just overwhelmed. Imagine being nineteen and having two babies at a place with no running water. Can you? I was not cut out for motherhood. My children were better off without me."

"Your sister told me she didn't think you had any children," Ren said. "Why didn't she know about them?"

"I was estranged from my family when I moved to the village. I didn't talk to any of them during that time. And once I left, I never even considered contacting them again."

This was a different image of the family than what Daisy had conveyed. Ren wasn't surprised. Estrangements of this kind often led to gilded and inaccurate memories. She had seen that a lot.

"So you took off. Where did you go?" Sean asked.

"To San Francisco, for a time. I know you may not believe this, Detective Lukela, but it was very difficult for me to leave. My heart was broken by my own incompetence. I needed God in my life, not the religion Tal was preaching. So I joined a convent in San Anselmo."

"But not as Dixie Larkin."

"No, I needed a clean break. Betty was this crazy woman who lived at Shadow Rock. You ever see people standing on street corners, talking to the heavens? That was Betty."

"So why did you steal her name?"

"I just needed a name to get by for a few years. I figured Betty was so far off the grid it was the safest one to use. But then I took to the convent life. I truly felt reborn there. I was a mess when I entered. I thought I was going to hell for abandoning my children. But I got stronger by grace. God forgave me. And he led me out of the darkness. I saw clearly that Shadow Rock forced into a role against my choice. I was not meant to be a mother. I was meant to help other girls like me."

"So you never ran into any trouble, forging this identity," Ren asked.

"No. There has been no challenge at all. If the real Betty Holland is still alive, she is still off the radar. But, then again, so am I. I don't even file tax returns."

"At what point did you realize your daughter was in Seattle?" Ren asked.

Betty looked at her lawyer, then across the table at the others. "You don't seem to understand, detectives. I don't have a daughter. She was never mine. God brought her into the world through me, but I was not meant to be her mother."

It was hard to know how much of this she really believed and how much of it was just the narrative she was feeding herself. Sean was getting annoyed with her. "You're not answering the question," he said.

"The only time I wondered was the first time I met you, Detective Lukela. When I saw the police sketch of the Capitol Hill murder victim, it looked a bit like me at that age. I suspected I couldn't come clean with you, even if I'd been sure it was her. I've worked so hard to put the past behind me."

"So you're telling us that you had no knowledge that Cedar was living in Seattle?" Ren asked.

"No, none."

"That sounds fanciful. She was looking for her biological mother."

"Maybe so, but it's the truth."

Leo Bassan interrupted them. "You have no DNA evidence connecting my client to the crime scene. She has told you she didn't know the victim. So unless you're going to charge her with something, I would like to see things wrap up."

Ren turned to Sister Betty and asked, "Did you have any contact with Ruby West?"

"Is that the other girl that died?"

"Yes. She grew up at Shadow Rock. She was a student at Pacific Community College."

"I remember her as a little girl. I knew her parents. But I've never met her as an adult."

"You never saw the website she had up about Shadow Rock?"

"I'm not really a web person."

"OK. So what you are saying is that you didn't know either of the girls that died."

"That's right," Sister Betty said. "I didn't know either of them."

They handed her a photo. Jesse West had given it to them. In it Ruby was dressed in a purple peasant top. Her hair was shaggy. She was wearing silver half-moon earrings.

"You've never seen this girl?" Ren asked her.

She looked at the photograph, then at the detectives. "No," Sister Betty said. "She doesn't look familiar to me."

CHAPTER TWENTY-SEVEN

Since New Year's Ren had added Jefferson's face to the Mount Rushmore puzzle. When she examined her project, three dead presidents looked out at her. She was just missing Washington. His face was piled up in pieces along with too much white granite and blue sky. She snapped a few pieces of baby blue together and then tossed them aside.

Technically, today was her day off. She had gone for a long run in the morning, taken Ariel to have her nails clipped, and cleaned out Puck's cage. The sun was out, and it was a warm day for January. She had a thick raw steak and bell peppers in her fridge that she was going to grill in a bit.

Ren had read the last part of Jesse West's statement many times. She was convinced the solution to the crime was somewhere in it.

Shortly before Cedar called last summer, Ruby showed an interest in doing a documentary about Shadow Rock. I was a little concerned when she brought the idea up. She had told me once that she had a memory as a little girl of having twin sisters and that one was taken away. She was remembering Cedar and Talia. They were the same age.

I lied to her and said that wasn't possible, but she wanted to investigate it. I discouraged her in every way I could, but she had moved out by then. Plus I trusted everyone at Shadow Rock, still. I knew they would keep our secret. We had forged birth certificates, and no one wanted the legal hassle.

Ruby came back from her trip, but she didn't tell me she had discovered anything. It seemed to me that she hadn't. She was more focused on getting an internship than the documentary. I never saw her website. She was very secretive about a lot of things. If I had known about it, I would have encouraged her to shut it down. She did not know what she was getting into.

That was the end of Jesse's statement, and it was a lot. The case seemed clearer by the day. Cedar Heekin had grown up knowing in her gut that that she was not her mother's daughter. She knew from her birth certificate that she was born in Eplin. Cedar took a trip to Shadow Rock. Somehow she got the impression that Lydia Merton was her mother. Some time after that, she found Lydia's thesis and got the name Jesse West. When he was uncooperative, she focused on trying to build a relationship with Lydia Merton. She got nowhere. She may have broken into Lydia's house looking for proof of their relationship.

Ruby West, haunted by a girlhood memory, was attempting to film a documentary that would solve the mystery. She had put up a website, teasing her audience that she knew this memory of hers was tied to the mysterious Capitol Hill case. Whatever her theory, it had died with her.

But even with all this critical information, there was still a sky-wide hole in the case. There had been two illegal adoptions, and forgery of birth certificates and identities. The parties were admitting their complicity with astonishing candor, now that the immunity offers were in.

But the piece that was still missing was the biggest: who had been driven, three times, to kill over all this?

CHAPTER TWENTY-EIGHT

Ren was just back from a run, dripping in sweat, when she passed over the railroad tracks and saw Milton Hutching standing on her porch. She gasped at the sight of him. It had been years since she had laid eyes on the man, but he hadn't changed. He was still huge and hulking, a grizzly bear.

Ren descended the stairs to the dock, trying to act calm. She had dealt with scarier scenarios than this. Milton had something in his hand, which he slipped into his pocket when he saw her.

"Mr. Hutching," she said. "I think I know I why you're here."

He turned and, to Ren's surprise, greeted her warmly. For a second she thought he was going to hug her. She was glad that her sweaty body was acting as a repellent.

"I heard about the break-in on your property. You're probably wondering why my fingerprints were found in your house. And that's a perfectly reasonable cause for concern."

"No, I figured that one out myself," Milton said. "I have some surveillance video of the two of you on my front porch in December."

Ren's heart sank. She was hoping that the front porch was the only place Milton stashed video cameras.

"I stopped by because I wanted to ask you if you know where Del is hiding herself these days. We came home, and she had cleared out again. I don't know why."

"I haven't seen her since that day I was at your house," Ren said. It was true. She had talked to Del twice by phone since that time, but that was it. It always helped when she could rely on the truth. "Do you think she's using again?"

Milton shrugged helplessly. For a second, Ren almost felt sorry for him. He was convincing playing the long-suffering father of an addict. He'd had years to hone the act.

"Can I count on you to keep your eyes and ears open?" he asked. "You've got the tools at your disposal."

"Of course I will," Ren said. She meant it too. It was a peculiar commonality they shared. They both wanted the best for Delphine; they just had different ideas about what the right thing was for her.

"Thanks a lot, kid," Milton said. "Next time, I'll call first. I was in the neighborhood. Looks like I'm interrupting your day off, so I'll be gone. Oh, and by the way, I told the detectives you are in the clear. They never had their doubts about you."

Ren watched him as he walked away. When she stepped in her living room, she realized she'd been fooled. She could smell his stench around her in the enclosed space. Even Ariel looked spooked. Milton had been on the boat; she was sure of it. He probably stole the key from Del and made a copy.

Luckily, though, Ren was a few steps ahead of him. There was nothing on the houseboat for him to find.

• • •

Ren was just out of the shower when the phone rang. Her nerves were still a bit frayed from the encounter with Milton. She had cracked a few windows, and the breeze was helping a bit. She was thinking a drink at Sanctuary was going to be a necessity tonight.

She answered her cell.

"I just got the news, Ren. Pacific Community College has reported Lydia Merton missing. She didn't show up for her first class of the new year. Someone from the school went to her house. Her mailbox was full, and her house seemed undisturbed. Her car was parked half a block down. A unit checked her house. She's not there."

Ren sat down on the couch, her hair dripping down her bare shoulders. After Jesse West's statement and the interview with Sister Betty Holland, the case was at a turning point. And, yet, they hadn't found their killer. Now it appeared they had another victim.

"If she's dead, it didn't happen at home. It's more like the boy that was dumped downtown. We don't have a consistent pattern with this killer."

"You think the deaths are unrelated?" Sean asked.

Ren was thinking about that day at the Aloha house and the artwork Del had shown her, how it showed no demonstrable pattern until you got to the right vantage point. This was true of detective work too: you had to see the evidence from just the right angle to properly understand it. Ren was starting to wonder if maybe they had been looking at this case in the wrong way.

"I've got an idea," she told her partner. "Meet me at the precinct as soon as you can get there."

"I've got my niece today, Ren. It might take me a while."

"That's fine. I'll see you when I see you."

• • •

When Sean arrived at the precinct, it was getting dark outside. The building was empty except for a security guard at the street entrance. All he could see as he approached was his partner sitting at her desk, looking over reports under yellow light.

"What is all this?" he asked her.

Ren's desk was covered with papers. She had been there for several hours. In front of her was a stacked printout. She was going over it with several different highlighters. She also had a day planner for 2011. She had written notes all over it: phone numbers and initials at certain times and certain days.

Jason Twick had had the unenviable task when the case began of going through Father David Skarda's phone records. There were no fewer than 700 numbers in a three-month period. Like many people in social services, Father Skarda knew hundreds of people. He talked to many of them regularly by phone.

"What are you looking for?" Sean said, peering over her shoulder.

"A pattern," Ren said.

He walked over to his desk and started warming up his computer. At this juncture, he wasn't even sure why she needed him. "This just came to you?"

"I was thinking about two things today," she said. "Obsession and vantage point. And something occurred to me, a new place to look."

It was true. She had been thinking about Milton's obsession with controlling Del and about the artwork Del had shown her. They were coalescing in her mind. She had a theory.

"How can I assist you in your efforts?" Sean asked.

"You could look up a phone number for me," she told him.

"You got it. Whose?"

"Air Canada," Ren said. "I need to request another flight manifest."

CHAPTER TWENTY-NINE

Father David Skarda unwrapped the fresh meat with a feeling of contentment. It was a six-pound roast, her favorite. He placed it on a cutting board with the potatoes, carrots, and onions. He went into the refrigerator and looked around. He hadn't thought to bring butter. She would probably have some in here somewhere. He opened the freezer. A pound of Tillamook, salted. He pulled it out.

He had already been to the wine rack and uncorked a bottle of pinot noir. It was a pricey vintage, but he was drinking it with gusto. It fed the blood. *Revolver* was on the stereo. She had bought it for him.

Father Skarda had read somewhere that the revolver was the only gun to leave no shell casings at crime scenes. It was a curiosity to him, then, that so few crimes seemed to be committed with them. He wondered if, on some level, killers wanted to leave their calling card.

He peeled the potatoes, then the carrots. He had bought a popover mix to make Yorkshire pudding. He didn't feel up to doing it from scratch tonight. He had skipped the dessert aisle too. In the last few weeks, he had noticed that his pants were a little snug. The new year was always the time to cut back.

Father Skarda took a sip of wine. He loved the stillness of a quiet house. He'd had so little of that in his life. He had gone to the seminary at twenty-one and had lived in group settings ever since. In fact, he had never lived on his own.

The CD stopped. He walked into the front room and selected another, Beth Orton's *Daybreaker*. He loved the opening track.

As he walked back toward the kitchen, he heard a key in the front door. It surprised him.

"You're home early," he said. He wasn't quite ready for her, but feigned enthusiasm.

"Not much going on today," she said, throwing her coat on the couch. They embraced for a moment, feeling the familiarity of years together.

"I even let Tish go home early," she said.

"Dinner won't be ready for a few hours," he said.

Fiona smiled with appreciation. She'd gotten used to this in their twenty years together. She didn't see him often, but when she did it was precious.

Once, they had been engaged. It was during their college days at Berkeley. Fiona wore cocktail dresses to class and had her thin hair waved like a '30s movie star. David thought she looked like Bette Davis. He was both ardent and tender in his pursuit of her. They traveled up and down the coast in Fiona's MG, happy to be away from all the crazies at Cal. One weekend during their junior year, he slipped a ring on her finger while they overlooked the rocks at Big Sur.

They had been engaged a few months when he told her he'd had a change of heart. He felt a pull to serve God. There was no option for him but Rome. It was the one true faith, at least for him. If the Vatican were behind the times on celibacy, it was still the moral authority in most other areas. He had found his calling.

They broke up for several years. When they both ended up back in their native Seattle, they reconnected. That was years ago now.

Fiona didn't hear from David often. He was meticulous in secrecy, insisting that they restrict phone time and meetings in public. He knew so many people in Seattle, and all it would take was one wagging tongue to make his life difficult.

Fiona went along with this. The truth was, she had no choice in the matter. Despite his life of service, David was also an inherently selfish man. When she objected, as she had quite often in their early years together, the implication was quite clear: she would either accept these rules or she would lose him.

So they carried on like this. Stolen moments like tonight, and a vacation together every April. This year it would be Key West. They would drink rum and read Hemingway and watch as the dolphins swam toward the horizon. She was already looking forward to it.

By the time the roast was sizzling, another bottle of pinot had been opened. A few years ago they had toured Napa Valley for their April trip. This was the last remnant. They sat in the dining room, enjoying their souvenir.

After a while, there was a knock on the door. They both looked at each other, surprised. Fiona had almost no friends. People didn't stop by, ever.

She walked over and answered the door. Father Skarda heard two voices talking to Fiona. She sounded tense in response. He walked over to see who it was.

A cold blast of air hit him as he entered the front room. Her heard a crack, a noise he had never heard before.

He moved quickly to get a clearer view. Fiona was in the doorway, under porch light. She was turned around, facing him, her hands pulled behind her. He spotted the detectives from the Capitol Hill case. They were talking to her.

Then he heard their words: "Fiona Swift, you are under arrest for the murders of Cedar Heekin and Ruby West.…"

CHAPTER THIRTY

Ren had been interviewing Fiona Swift for four hours, but she still wasn't giving it up. She'd pulled out all the usual tricks: threats that she would end up at Walla Walla, countered with offers of sending her to a more humane prison. She had lied and told her that Father David Skarda was the one who had turned her in. Fiona didn't believe it.

Sean sat in the next room, doing a similar routine with Father Skarda. His testimony was going to be critical to getting a conviction. Thus far, it was an uphill battle. He didn't believe it when Sean told him that Lydia Merton was missing. It was true he hadn't seen her since before Christmas, but it was not unusual that they went weeks without contact. He saw no cause for concern.

This is what they had: Air Canada had provided manifests that showed that Fiona and David had been on the same flights more than once. One trip, in April 2011, was to Quebec City. Two years before that they went to Vancouver, also in April. The detectives had procured hotel receipts with Fiona Swift's name on them, at romantic getaway spots. The room service bills showed large amounts of food, but otherwise David Skarda's thumbprint was absent.

They also had phone records showing that David and Fiona talked occasionally, sometimes late at night. However, the calls were scarce and were found amidst hundreds the priest made, many to female parishioners.

There was also the matter of Ruby West. They had proof that Fiona Swift and Ruby West worked together. Fiona had let Ruby link her site about Shadow Rock to her website. They also had proof that Fiona had read Ruby's site at 5 p.m. on December 20. Shortly thereafter she had Googled her address.

There were no signs of forced entry at Ruby's apartment. She had most likely opened her front door to someone she knew, who then killed her. There was also the text on Ruby's website. She had posted the first in a planned series of investigative pieces about the Capitol Hill murder. In the first, Ruby claimed to have insider knowledge of who had committed the crime. She named no names, but promised by the end of the series to reveal the truth.

All of this evidence had been enough to arrest Fiona Swift.

Ren and Sean believed that Fiona saw the text on Ruby's website and thought that Ruby was onto her. She went over to Ruby's apartment, and Ruby let her inside. Fiona killed her to cover her tracks.

But they weren't kidding themselves. This theory lacked many crucial links. There was nothing linking Fiona Swift to the boy that was found shot downtown. A good defense attorney would argue the murder/suicide angle and claim that Fiona was being framed because of her connection to Ruby West.

The linchpin was Father David Skarda. If they could get him to turn on her and reveal information about their affair, they would be that much closer.

Thus far in the interview, Fiona had denied knowing about Skarda's relationship with Lydia. She admitted Googling Ruby's address on the day she was killed, but claimed that it was because Ruby had forgotten her letter of recommendation when she left her internship. Fiona was planning to mail it to her and had looked up the information. She admitted reading Ruby's website on the day she died but said that she thought her intern was just blowing smoke about the case. She was certain from their work together that the girl knew nothing about who killed Cedar. Fiona had spent four hours with Ren protesting her innocence. The police were simply wrong in arresting her.

Ren took a break as the fifth hour started. Sean joined her in the hallway outside the interview rooms.

"What do you think?" Sean said. He was deferring to Ren a lot. He was feeling a mix of awe and pride that she had figured this out.

"She's really good, Sean. She has a plausible explanation for every bit of evidence I've got. She's going to be really convincing in front of a jury."

"So what do we do?"

"Skarda is our best bet. We've got to get him to turn on her. If he loves Lydia at all, the knowledge that Fiona has killed her might turn him."

"So far he doesn't believe what I'm telling him. He's really been fooled by that woman."

Ren was feeling slightly sick thinking about Lydia. If she had been a believer, she would have said a prayer for her safe return.

"Tell me again, how did you crack this?" Sean asked.

"Once I realized I'd been looking in the wrong place, I got to thinking. Del told me this story once about her father and stepmother. Christiana came into Del's room one night when she was a girl. She told her that she thought Milton was having an affair. She dragged her into her car, and they drove up to Magnolia. Del said they sat there in her car, spying on this house, waiting to catch Milton in the act. At one point, a woman came to the front door. Del said they could see her just in shadow. And Christiana freaked out and took off. She just didn't have the courage to meet the woman Milton was cheating on her with."

"But how do you get from that to Cedar Heekin dying?" Sean asked.

"It got me to thinking...maybe Father Skarda had another mistress. Maybe she was like Christiana: she had stalked the house but hadn't confronted Lydia in person," she said. "And, what if, she finally gets up the nerve, goes to the house, only to find Cedar Heekin there?"

Sean still hadn't put it all together. Why would someone kill Cedar in Lydia's stead?

"I'm thinking that the death was an accident," Ren said. "Fiona went there to confront her, scare her."

"But she was stabbed."

Ren laughed. "Did I mention there are still a few holes in this theory of mine? But it's coming into focus. We're closer than we've ever been."

"I think you should talk to Skarda," Sean said. "Let's mix this up for a bit and see if we have better results."

Ren looked at him, emboldened. It was a good suggestion, and she accepted it gratefully.

As they walked down the hall, parting for their separate rooms, Ren turned to her partner and said, "Sean, please don't leave your job because of what happened last Christmas."

"How did you know I was thinking of leaving?" Sean asked.

There had never been a good moment to discuss it. Now was as good as any. "Stella Hadley coughed it up. She's taking martial arts at your sister's studio."

He looked puzzled. Then he said, "And so are you apparently."

Ren blushed. One of these days she's spill the beans about her crush on his sister. It never was the right time. She'd been feeling it a bit ever since Sean's barbecue last July. "I don't care what Conlin does to us. We can't let him win. I need you to be my partner."

Sean smiled. "You don't need me, Ren. But I tell you what. Crack the priest, and I'm not going anywhere."

They exited into separate rooms.

Two hours later, Father David Skarda turned on Fiona Swift.

• • •

In the last hours of her life, Lydia Merton saw a red *torii* amidst lush pine trees. She smelled salt in the air and could taste eel. She felt a pearl rosary in her hand and the cobblestones of a medieval terra cotta village under her feet.

The last image she saw was a shaft of white light, bolder and brighter than any she had seen. There was darkness too, casting shadows amidst the white. The colors moved together until she couldn't tell between them.

And finally the words: *Seattle Police. We are here to help you.*

• • •

December 20, 2011

It was a few days before Christmas, and Ruby West couldn't help but feel giddy. She had just completed an internship with Swift Crime Productions, with a reference that bolstered her chances of getting into Columbia Film School. She wasn't sure anymore that she wanted to go. She was starting to think that investigative journalism was her bag.

She had spent the day baking, a few of her father's favorites. She had set the fire alarm off twice. Ordinarily she never opened the windows in her apartment. Lily, her tabby cat, was an escape artist who wanted nothing more than to gain precious freedom via the fire escape. Today the smell of burnt cookies was too much to bear, however. She had opened her bedroom window. Lily was currently locked inside the bathroom, meowing unhappily.

Now, as the day gave way to darkness, Ruby was once again reading the copy on her website. She had put it up several hours before. There had already been over two hundred views. She kept taking breaks to read it again and see the attention it was getting.

• • •

A Tale of Two Girls

Tongues have been wagging for months now. How did a young woman, a runaway, end up dead in the house of Lydia Merton? Is Lydia really as innocent as she claims? Police have their theories; journalists have their theories. So far they're both wrong.

I am about to take you on a journey. You will be a different person when this four-part series is over. You will wonder how it is police have messed this up. You will know why an innocent girl died.

The problem, dear reader, is that the detectives never found me.

She had named no names yet. But Ruby had a theory. As a girl Ruby had a memory of twin sisters at Shadow Rock. They were a few years younger than she. One day a woman showed up and kidnapped one of them.

Although she had no proof yet, Ruby believed that Lydia Merton had uncovered this mystery while doing her thesis at Shadow Rock. Someone had threatened her, though, so she now distanced herself from what she knew. Cedar had broken into Lydia's house to try to find out the mystery of why she had been taken from Shadow Rock as a baby.

Ruby had encountered a nun named Sister Betty Holland who

was clearly hiding something. Ruby thought that Sister Betty may have killed Cedar to hide her secret past.

It was true that the theory was speculative, but Ruby was certain she had come close to cracking the case. She was excited about posting the next entry but would wait a while. Suspense was all about timing, she found.

Ruby walked into the kitchen. It was a mess, but she couldn't quite deal with it yet.

There was a knock on the door. Ruby wasn't surprised. She had been expecting a drop-in from her building manager ever since the second fire alarm went off. She walked over and swung the door open.

Standing in the hallway was Fiona Swift.

Ruby's heart accelerated. She glanced furtively at her computer screen, still opened to her website.

Fiona smiled at her. "You're a clever girl," she said. "But did it not occur to you that I can help you with this scoop?"

Ruby smiled back. She was surprised. She had been expecting Fiona to be furious when and if she discovered her deception.

"May I come in for a moment?" Fiona said. "I think we can strike a deal that we're both happy with."

Ruby let her in, shutting the door behind her. Lily was meowing deeply and scratching at the bathroom door. Ruby walked over and let Lily out. She raced out, happy.

Ruby turned her attention back to Fiona. Actually, she didn't see Fiona. All she saw was the barrel of a gun.

"You're going to disable that site now," Fiona said.

Ruby didn't argue. She was terrified. She sat down at her desk. It took a while, but soon it was gone.

"Good," Fiona said. "I better not find that piece of yours anywhere else. You are done with your days as an amateur sleuth."

"OK," Ruby said. She had shut it down for real. Looking at a gun will do that to you.

"Give me the computer too," she said. Ruby did as she was told, unplugging the laptop and handing it to Fiona. It was so heavy she nearly dropped it as she gave it over.

Fiona put the gun back into her shoulder bag. It was unregistered, but she had had no intention of using it.

"Now," Fiona said. "Tell me what you know."

Ruby talked for a while, about her research and theories. Fiona listened intently.

Finally Fiona spoke: "Do you think I'm stupid?"

Ruby was flabbergasted. She had told her everything she knew. Her gut instinct, now that she had a moment to recover from the gun trauma, was to run. She darted past Fiona to the apartment door, but something hit her forcefully as she passed. Ruby lost consciousness before she could realize it was the laptop that had struck her: Fiona had hit her in the back of the head with it.

When Ruby hit the ground, her body was half in the bathroom. Blood was beginning to pool on the linoleum. Fiona pushed Ruby forward by her legs until her entire body was near the tub. Then she pulled her by her arms and dumped her in the claw-foot tub. She looked at the girl. She was not breathing.

Fiona had seen this before. It was fatal bleeding. She looked herself over: her trench coat was smeared with blood. She removed it carefully, turned it inside out, and placed the coat in her shoulder bag, along with the gun and the laptop. Fiona did not notice that the tip of her shoe was meeting a lip of blood on the floor.

From behind her, the tabby cat had run into the bathroom. It was bleating with fear and running around with great agitation.

Fiona left the apartment. The only sound she heard as she exited the building was the cat wailing good-bye.

October 24, 2011

Fiona Swift was a businesswoman by trade, successful in a field where few women ever dipped their toes. This gave her a slight air of cockiness at times. She always picked the location when meeting clients. It was as much about her aesthetic as it was her clients' needs. Tonight it was a deserted bar in Pioneer Square. The interior had checkerboard tiles and weathered leather booths lining a wall. There was a bartender who spoke no English. That was the way it needed to be.

She arrived early, as she always did. She selected the last booth before the room gave way to a ballroom-style dance floor. Swing bands played here on Saturday nights, patrons lindy hopping in vintage clothing. They were doing a special Day of the Dead–themed ball the next weekend. There were signs for it in the foyer.

Fiona sat, facing outward, toward the door. She ordered a whisky sour when the bartender stopped by. He knew what she liked. She had been here before.

Her client was late. Ordinarily that was a deal breaker, but this time she would wait. He was different. She checked her watch and opened her briefcase. She was prepared for tonight.

At 10:15 her client arrived. She had talked to him a few times on the phone at the office, and he had promised insider information about Lydia Merton. When he appeared, she was slightly taken aback. He was young, with spiky red hair and glasses. He was wearing a jean jacket and an orange T-shirt. Fiona wasn't sure she recognized the logo.

"I love this," he said, slipping into the booth opposite her. "So cloak and dagger."

Fiona wasn't amused. Her eyes darted around the bar. It was deserted tonight. It catered to a weekend crowd, but had lost a lot of business since Sanctuary opened a few years ago. "You said you have information about our client," Fiona said. She always used this lingo in public.

Jakob grinned. He was prepared to earn a little money while having some fun with Lydia. He knew about her relationship with Father Skarda. She thought she was being secretive, but it hadn't taken much to figure it out. And since the body had turned up in Lydia's house, he was sure the killing had something to do with the priest. He had a theory about the case.

Jakob filled Fiona in on what he knew—about his relationship with Lydia and hers with a priest named David Skarda. Fiona took it all in, impassive. She had to figure out what this kid knew before she decided what to do.

Fiona was still in shock about what had happened the previous week. When she left the house on Capitol Hill a week ago, she had thought she had killed Lydia Merton. When she got home, she stood under the shower spray sobbing. She hadn't meant to kill her. Lydia was her romantic rival, and she wanted to confront her about it. That was all.

Fiona's phone started ringing later that night. Her sources were giving her a tip about a murder on Capitol Hill. This wasn't unusual. She got calls like this any time there was significant police activity.

But then there was more. Reports were that the young woman who died had broken into the property. The owner of the home had come back to find her dead on the floor.

Fiona was aghast when she realized her mistake. But she was also sure of one thing: she simply could not get caught for what she did. She had done enough interviews with inmates who were hollow inside. Prison was worse than death. She would do whatever it took to cover her tracks.

The best solution was for her to cover the story as she normally would, albeit with the urgent focus of trying to figure out what police and other journalists knew.

She hadn't factored on the kid. He had found her. He was a student at Pacific Community College. He told her he was Lydia's lover and that he had a theory of the murder.

"Tell me your theory," Fiona said now. She had the urge for a cigarette.

"I think the church killed her," Jakob said. He seemed excited, as if this were entertainment to him. "They knew about the affair between Lydia and Skarda, and they put a hit on her. What they didn't factor on was that she was out of town the night the killer was sent. The assassin found the homeless girl instead. It was an accident that she was the one killed."

Fiona tapped her hand on the table. She took another swig of her drink. She hadn't figured on this at all. The kid had about 85% of the story right, and he was clearly eager to talk to the press about it.

"A deal's a deal, Mr. Hekking. If you can offer me exclusive rights to this information, I will pay you for it."

Jakob grinned. "I haven't told anyone. This is big, right?"

Fiona smiled. "It is, Jakob." She waved over the bartender. Tomorrow she would offer him a generous envelope of cash with the promise she wouldn't turn him in to the INS. It would keep him quiet if Jakob's death made the papers.

"We can work this out at my office tomorrow," Fiona told Jakob. "Now I'm wondering if you might walk me to my car. This neighborhood is sketchy at this time of night. No one outside but winos and rats."

She paid the bill, and they walked in silence. They could see their breath. When they reached her Lexus SUV, she stopped. She had parked on a side street under an overpass.

"Can I give you a ride, maybe?" she asked. "The buses are infrequent in this neighborhood."

"That'd be great," Jakob said. He opened the passenger door and got in. Fiona walked around to the driver's side. She had only a moment to get this right. She pulled the gun out of her briefcase and got into the car. She aimed at his temple. He never saw it coming.

She drove frantically until she found a deserted part of the underpass. She stopped the car, opened his door, and let the body fall. She wiped the gun and dropped it near him. Later, she would come *back with some of Cedar's things. It was the best she could do to make this look like a murder-suicide. First up, she needed to clean the inside of her car. It was a mess.*

Fiona raced home, her pulse beating wildly. She couldn't believe what she'd done. But she felt a cold quality coming over her again. She would do what she needed to do to survive.

October 13, 2011

Cedar Heekin watched the blood and gore, mesmerized. She had only seen a few episodes of True Blood, and she wasn't sure she liked it. Vampires just weren't her thing. Still, it beat all the cooking shows Lydia TiVo'd. Or worse, British detective shows. Who watched such things?

It had taken Cedar months to work up the nerve to be here. She had made contact with Lydia for the first time the previous April, when she had written her a letter. She had just gotten back from a trip to Shadow Rock. While she was there a woman named Maude Rasmussen had told her about her mother. Maude had been so kind that Cedar almost wished she were her mother. But she told her about Lydia, and Cedar left California with a mission to meet her. As soon as she was home, she ran her name through Google and found her at the PCC website.

Secretly she had hoped that this was all it would take. One small gesture, and she imagined the starting point of a growing relationship between herself and Lydia. Some part of her knew that this was a fantasy, but still she hoped.

She had been disappointed. The letter she had gotten back from Lydia was polite but curt. She had not, as Cedar had hoped, initiated any further contact.

After that, Cedar had found a thesis that Lydia wrote online. She had only skimmed the first part, because time on a computer was hard to come since she had left home. But she had found a man in Seattle who had spent time there and seemed to know Lydia. She had tried to talk to him but been rebuffed. She'd had more luck talking to his daughter. She was nice, but didn't know much about either Lydia or Shadow Rock.

Her efforts to get to know Lydia Merton had stalled, but she had one other plan.

Cedar had had the fantasy for some time of breaking into Lydia's house. It wouldn't be that difficult. She knew where she lived, and from her time canvassing the neighborhood she knew it was sparsely populated during certain times of the day and darkly lit at night after people had gone to bed.

Cedar had broken into homes before. The key was getting to know the area first and trying to get to know the owner's schedule. She knew from the Pacific Community College website that Lydia was busy there on Mondays and Tuesdays, but the rest of her week was largely open.

Lydia also went to campus a lot on Saturdays.

Cedar's plan was simple: break into the house and have a look. She hoped she might find something, anything, to help her better understand this woman who brought her into the world. Maybe a journal. She had the fantasy that Lydia might have written letters to her. "To my darling daughter," they would begin, heartfelt confessions of how hard it had been to give her up.

Even knowing what she wanted to do, it still took a lot of nerve to do it. Cedar finally had the courage the second weekend in October. She was tired of life on the streets, which for her often translated into sweet-talking men into letting her stay with them. Cedar was tired of men in general, tired of hustling. She was almost tempted to go back to Bridge. Her stepfather hated her, but he might let her back. He was a strange guy with a terrible temper, but Cedar had known worse men.

But first, Cedar was willing to try this. She went on Saturday at 10 a.m., which she had observed was the time Lydia often left the house, driving away in her forest-green Subaru.

When Cedar showed up that day, the house seemed quiet. She walked to the alley and made her way to the backyard. It was easy getting into the yard; the gate had been left unlocked. She looked around a bit. The neighborhood was quiet.

She moved quickly, shattering the glass to the back door with a rock. There were some shards that Cedar had to get around, but it was relatively easy to unlock the door from the angle of the window. She nicked her hand and sucked on it to quell the blood. But before she knew it, she was inside the basement.

Cedar's heart raced as she got her bearings. She was quiet, listening for signs of life. She inched up the stairs, prepared to bolt at the first sign of life. The door to the kitchen, which was up the stairs from the basement, was unlatched. Cedar moved inside, getting more confident as she moved room from room. There was no sign of Lydia.

Cedar looked around, staying away from the windows in front—not that it mattered, necessarily. This was the city, where neighbors were strangers. Cedar looked into a first floor room. It had a bed and bookcases, and also a messy desk. A computer had been left on. Next to it, on the printer, papers were cascading out. A few had fallen to the floor.

Cedar picked up the printouts. One was a boarding pass for Air Canada, for a flight earlier that day. The papers had Lydia's name on them. Another was an itinerary, with flights, hotel, and rental car information. It appeared that Lydia had flown out of Seattle earlier that day, bound for Alberta. She would be gone until Thursday night.

Cedar felt like she had won the jackpot. She was now in this luxurious home, with Lydia gone for five days. Cedar checked the Pacific Community College website. They were on fall break; classes were canceled M-W of the next week.

Cedar next checked the Air Canada website. The flight had taken off.

Cedar was golden. She had squatted in abandoned property before. This was slightly more dangerous, but she also was seeing it for the blessing it was.

Over the next few days, Cedar considered leaving. The house was cold; she couldn't figure out how to use the thermostat. Her main disappointment was that she couldn't find anything of the private side of Lydia. She kept no journals, no letters, and few personal photos. The best Cedar had was a tapestry coat that she had found in the downstairs closet. She loved the pattern. It fit like a glove. Cedar wore it indoors to fight off the chill, like a queen in a cloak. It, and the letter she had from her, were the only things that made her feel connected to her mother.

By Wednesday, Cedar was feeling ready to leave. She was taking no chances with Lydia being due back the next day. But first she'd finish with True Blood. There was one more episode after this one. Cedar was hungry as she watched. She'd been down to Broadway a few times to get food. She liked Pagliacci.

Cedar hit pause mid-episode and grabbed some money, a ten, from her backpack on the couch. She left the house. She had the coat on; she was seldom without it. It was easy enough to slip in and out. The front door didn't lock when it was shut; you had to do that manually. That meant that Cedar could leave by the front door and get back in, all without a key.

Cedar walked down to Broadway, moving quickly. She was hungry and eager to get back to the episode. She ordered the #4 at Pagliacci: Spinach Ricotta Lasagna. She paid with a ten that she had in her pocket and only got back change.

Walking home, Cedar smelled the warm garlic bread wafting toward her. She was ravenous. She opened the box and ate a piece of bread. She pulled a layer off the spinach lasagna. She bit into it. It was so hot she spit part of it back out. Hot pasta and cheese spilled down the front of the jacket. "Fuck!" she screamed, as angry about the lost food as the damage to the coat.

By the time Cedar reached 21st Avenue, it was getting dark. She was not aware of the woman watching her from a parked car.

Fiona had been here a few times since she discovered the photograph. It was in David's satchel. She had snooped when he was in the shower. Amidst papers and his cell phone, she had found it in an inside pocket. It was a photograph of a woman, age about twenty-three. She was wearing a tapestry coat and nothing else. She sat, the coat barely covering her naked body and breasts. She was looking down, her strawberry blonde hair cascading over her. On the back of the photograph she had written:

David
You and no other.
Lydia

Fiona was amazed at David's thoughtlessness. A man of such scrupulous secrecy, limiting his calls with Fiona to one a month at most, refusing to be seen in public with her. His entire life was about not getting caught. Why had he carried this photo with him? Maybe he had forgotten it was there. Or maybe, on some sick level, he wanted Fiona to know about this woman. Fiona was no fool. She knew that she wasn't quite enough woman for David. Maybe he was looking for a way out.

Still, Fiona was shocked to discover this deception. David was the only man she had ever been with. She believed him when he told Fiona that he considered her his wife. They would be married were it not for Rome.

After she discovered the photo, Fiona started to stalk David a bit. He was so busy, with so many appointments, that she almost gave up her efforts. But one night she had trailed him to this house. He had entered via the back. He was carrying a bag of groceries from Morello's, their favorite market. He probably had a bag of Italian imports and free-range meat, all for her.

Fiona had driven away with tears stinging her eyes. She wasn't sure she could face this woman. She drove by again a few days later. She walked up to her porch with the intention of knocking, but had second thoughts. She was certain from the photo that Lydia was a looker. Probably sexy as hell. Fiona couldn't handle it. Instead she had peered into the mailbox. The woman's last name was Merton. Lydia Merton. Even her name was sexy.

Recently Fiona had felt greater courage. David had been calling her less, dropping by less. She hadn't seen him much that year at all, apart from the trip to Quebec City. She feared she was losing him for good to Lydia.

This week she lay in wait. She watched Lydia come and go a few times. She was wearing the same coat from the photo, walking somewhere and coming back with food.

Today she came back about five. She had a white box of food with her. She rounded the corner and approached her house. Fiona exited her car and rushed across the street to catch her.

"Lydia?" Fiona said.

Cedar looked behind her. A woman was standing on the pavement sidewalk leading to the house.

"Are you Lydia?" The woman asked.

"Yes," Cedar said. "I'm Lydia." She instantly regretted saying it. It felt so false. But she hadn't had time to deliberate.

"My name is Fiona Swift," the woman said. "Perhaps you've seen me on the news? I'm a crime reporter. May I come in and talk to you for a moment?" She flashed a press pass.

Cedar nodded, intrigued. She opened the front door. There were noises inside: screaming, Southern accents. Cedar had hit pause on TiVo before she left, and it had popped back. The TV was blaring.

They entered the house. Cedar removed the tapestry coat and threw it down the laundry chute, which she had discovered earlier that day. Cedar walked to the back room to turn off the TV. She switched it off and placed her food box near the couch.

She turned to face the woman.

"I realize that what I'm about to say to you might be a huge shock," Fiona began. Cedar watched her, mesmerized. She couldn't make out a lot of it, except that this woman was involved with a priest and seemed to think Lydia was too.

Cedar was positively fascinated. Was it possible her father was a priest? Maybe this was why Lydia had abandoned her. In her mind's eye, Cedar imagined the three of them: Lydia, the priest, and herself: a family at last. Her lips tugged into a smile.

Fiona stopped mid-sentence, looking at Lydia. Up until now, she had been pretty even-handed. She had talked about her twenty-year relationship with David, their love, and how much it meant to her.

Lydia had said nothing in response. But now the bitch was smiling at her. She was smug, mocking.

Fiona felt anger surge in her. She lunged at Lydia, knocking her backward. She heard a crack that shocked her. Lydia had smacked her head against a marble end table near the red couch. She had fallen on her back, knocked out. Blood was gushing from her head.

Fiona watched the scene, horrified. She hadn't realized until the lunge just how slight Lydia was. She was really just a girl.

Fiona saw Lydia's eyes open. A bubble broke on her lips. Then she stopped breathing.

Fiona was aghast. What had she done? She stood there for a few moments, frozen.

After a moment, her mind was calm. She had just killed a woman, her romantic rival. Her DNA might be at the scene. Her only goal now was to not get caught.

She didn't dare take her pulse for fear of leaving something behind. Fiona moved calmly to the kitchen. She looked through the drawers, pulling out a large knife. She went back into the TV room. She stabbed the body three times to make sure she was dead.

Blood was on Fiona's hand. In haste, she hadn't thought what she'd do with the knife once she was done with it. There was an opened backpack on the couch, a woven soft side. Fiona reached for it. She stuffed the bloody knife inside. She would take it with her.

Fiona looked at the body one last time. Lydia's eyes were now open, staring at the ceiling.

There was no doubt now that Lydia Merton was dead. She had murdered her.

EPILOGUE

It was Mardi Gras at Sanctuary, and that meant a costume party and fruity cocktails heavy on the Southern Comfort and Herbsaint. Ramon was behind the bar, dressed in a Knights of Columbus costume. He had Puck on his shoulder. He leaned over and strained a pink cocktail into a chilled martini glass.

"For our departing friend," he said. He placed a plate and fork on the bar near the drink. "And why don't you try some Quiche Bebe with that."

Sean took a bite and smiled contentedly.

"Don't eat too much of that," Ren said. "I don't want you getting sick again."

Sean shook his head. He would never live that down. "You're really not at all curious how I figured out Pablo's father?" he asked his partner.

Ren shook her head. "Not even."

"I am," Ramon said, lifting the parrot off his shoulder and putting him on the bar. Puck wobbled like a drunken man down the surface. "Tell me."

"Lieutenant Roemer told me on the way home from the Christmas party," Sean said. "I heard all about the sperm bank and IVF. That's how I knew."

"Outstanding detective skills, my friend," Ramon said. "My tax dollars at work."

The men exchanged high fives.

From behind, a shower of colored beads flew over them. They scattered onto the bar, just missing the bird. "Babies!" Bebe called, throwing her arms around Ren and Sean from behind. She seemed to be hitting the Steel Magnolias extra hard tonight. "Are you excited for your trip?" she asked, taking a seat next to them.

They stayed silent for a few moments, not sure whom Bebe was addressing. They were both leaving for vacation in the next twenty-four hours: Sean was going home to Oahu tomorrow to see his parents, and Ren was taking her first trip abroad. She still couldn't believe her good fortune. Air Canada had comped her a ticket anywhere they flew. She was going to New Zealand, her first trip out of the country. Her bags were packed in the Camaro outside. Her flight to Sydney left at ten that night with a connecting flight to Queenstown. Ren would be back in time for the start of Fiona Swift's pretrial hearing, which was scheduled to begin the third week of March.

"I want you to promise me you aren't going to think about work while you're gone," Bebe said to Ren. "Puck and Ariel are with me, your case is closed, and that dreadful rich girl is out of your life again. Plus Lydia Merton is safe. I saw her interviewed on the news last night."

It was true: A SWAT team had found Lydia Merton in a cabin on Vashon Island belonging to Fiona Swift. She was hallucinating and near death from dehydration but was alive. After she recovered, Lydia told police about being abducted by Fiona Swift on Christmas Day and about being kept in the basement of her cabin for over two weeks. Her testimony was going to be pivotal at the upcoming pretrial hearing.

Between Lydia and Father Skarda's testimonies, the case was looking fairly strong. The priest would testify about their affair and about the fact that a photo he had of Lydia, taken early in their relationship, had gone missing from his things. Police had found the photo among Fiona's belongings. They believed she thought Lydia was a much younger woman than she was. This, and Cedar's presence at the house, had led to the mistaken killing.

And, in a forensic coup, trace amounts of blood and DNA from a Pacific Community College student named Jakob Hekking had been found in Fiona's car. At last they had an identity for the dead boy. He had placed two phone calls to Fiona's office shortly before his death. Police believed that he knew something about the crime and was blackmailing her. The case was not airtight, but Fiona was surely going away for something.

"That poor woman," Bebe said. "To be betrayed like that by the man she loved for so long. And then to go through a kidnapping."

Lydia certainly had been through a lot. She might even still be facing obstruction charges for not disclosing key bits of evidence to police. Dixie Larkin would likely see some jail time for fraud and identity theft, and Fiona Swift was looking at first- and second-degree murder charges, as well as kidnapping. This was a big case for the DA, and many would be paying for it. Ren would testify against any of the principals, but beyond that her role in the case was now over. It was time to move on.

"Have you been following all these news specials?" Bebe asked. Her TiVo was overloaded.

Ren shook her head. She was still not at liberty to talk about any details of the case that weren't public. She and Sean were avoiding the media until they testified at the upcoming pretrial. Time away was a blessed thing at moments like this.

"*48 Hours* hired this student from Berkeley to be a special consultant for the trial," Bebe continued. "He was the one who posted Lydia's thesis online originally. He was just a student at the time, hunting down sources on cults. He found some pack-rat professor who had Lydia's thesis. That's how he got it. He thought it might be of interest, so he posted it."

"Mom, I think you just tampered with a witness. Keep it up, and I'll turn you in."

Bebe laughed and then jumped down off her seat. She headed over to talk to a man dressed like the pope.

"Promise me something, Ren," Sean said. He was eating the last crumbs off his plate. "You're not going to ask my sister out unless you're serious about her, right? You've got Keala to consider."

Ren still couldn't believe how cool her partner was being about the news. "I'm not going to mess with anyone's child-hood," she told him. "I know better than that."

The truth was, Ren wasn't sure what would happen with Pearl. She had two weeks down under to make up her mind about her next move. And if there was one thing she had learned from this case, it was that a lot could happen in a few weeks.

Ren took a sip from her drink. She still had Del's note in her pocket. She had been carrying it with her since that day she came back from Eplin and found it on her bed, right near the pillow Del used to sleep on.

You know me. I can't stay. If you're ever in Anchorage, look up Jude Hamlin. And ask Pearl out, will ya? She would be the lucky one.

Ren had read the note so many times it was a mantra, an elegy. Del was gone again, possibly for good. Ren had done her a favor before she left: researching the case of Jude Hamlin, who had been missing for nearly ten years. Most likely Jude had died of an overdose and no one had claimed her body. Ren had found no living family on record and no death certificate.

That was all the information Del needed to buy Jude's identification from a dealer on the black market. Ren would turn a blind eye, as she always did to Del's shenanigans. Like

Dixie Larkin many years ago, Del wanted a fresh start. Ren was willing to give her one.

Ren finished her cocktail. She was limiting herself to one tonight. She felt a strange need to jet off alone for her first foreign trip. She couldn't wait to drive to the airport by herself and chat up a stranger on the plane.

As it neared departure time, Ren looked around Sanctuary. In the corner, Bebe was examining the jukebox, trying to find a suitable chaser to "And the Saints Go Marching In." Ramon was mixing cocktails, chattering to Sean about Moloka'i. Puck was on the bar, playing with a string of colored beads.

Ren pulled her coat around her, hopped down from the barstool, and headed out.

No one noticed she was gone.

THE END

ABOUT THE AUTHOR

Alex Nichols was born in a Mississippi River town, a speck on the map famous for producing a certain Gen X actress with a fondness for five-fingered discounts. She holds degrees from Smith College and the Graduate Theological Union, and currently lives in San Francisco.